SAINT'S FALL

BROTHERHOOD PROTECTORS WORLD

KATE MCKEEVER

Every book I write is dedicated to my mother and father. Though both are no longer with me now, I still have their love, support and pride in my memories of them. Without them, I wouldn't be the person, or writer, I am today. Thanks, Mom and Dad.

1

"I need your help."

Luc held the phone away from his ear and studied the caller ID for a second before responding. "Hank?"

"Yeah. You free for a few days or more?"

Hank Patterson was the one person Luc would never expect to call him, much less asking for assistance. "What's up? Something wrong with Hannah?"

"No. She's good, so is the ranch. I need you for something else."

Luc walked to the bar that served as his dining area and sat on a stool then rested his elbow on the laminate surface. "Okay, I'm listening."

"When did you serve in the Middle East? And what company were you in?" After Luc filled him in, Hank responded, a tone of relief in his voice. "I thought so. Look, I need to talk to you at some length. Can we hook up face to face?"

Luc shifted, suddenly aware of the ache in his left shoulder. "You mean me come out there or you come here?" Louisiana was a hell of a distance from Montana and Eagle

Rock. Besides, he didn't have a whole lot of good memories of the place, other than the rehab professionals that had brought him back from a black hole.

"No, at least not yet. Do you have a laptop or PC? We could do a face to face that way."

"Yeah, the 'new normal'," Luc muttered and heard an answering chuff of laughter from Hank. "Give me about ten minutes to get set up and contact me." He rattled of his contact information before disconnecting the call. He stood from the stool and, with a grunt of annoyance, headed for the bathroom and the extra strength aspirin he hoped would help deal with the phantom pain and aches of the day.

Ten minutes later, he had his laptop set up, a cup of coffee in his hand and leaned back in the recliner, his laptop on a TV tray. As he sipped his drink, he wondered what the devil Hank Patterson could want with him. Even if the Brotherhood Protector CEO believed in helping other vets out and hired them exclusively for his security firm, he didn't have any need for a man with one arm. Hell, Luc couldn't even do the one thing that had always provided him with stress relief, ride his bike, let alone work a security job. He muttered a curse; it was happening again. He could feel the dark hole trying to swallow him up. He brought up his email to waste some time before the call and spent a couple minutes responding to friends' emails. Why hadn't he come to this event? What was he doing now? When was he coming to visit the old neighborhood? He shifted in his seat, wishing for Hank to call him, get him out of the hole.

A trill of sound pulled him out of his thoughts and gratefully, he opened the page and found himself face to face with not only Hank Patterson, but Cole, his old counselor from Brighter Days Rehabilitation Ranch.

"Hey, man! How you doing?" Cole grinned as he greeted Luc.

"Not bad. You taking care of yourself and Van?"

Cole chuckled, "As much as I can. She's in South America, following a story about forest restoration."

"Well at least she's not following a terrorist group." Cole's wife, Vanessa, had been taken prisoner by a terrorist group when she worked as a free-lance reporter. After being released and showing up at the rehab ranch, she and Cole, in spite of both their resistance, had ended up together. And together, they were stronger than each had been apart.

"I think I've persuaded her to stick with the environmental issues for now. She's pretty passionate about the whole thing." Cole nodded.

"Give her my best when you see her." Luc said.

"Could be a bit. I'm not sure about the travel restrictions, but I'll pass on your message when we talk tonight." Cole rubbed his forehead, a gesture Luc remembered from a year ago when he'd been one of the sources of Cole's frustration.

"Okay, everyone said hello and how are ya." Hank shifted in his chair and frowned at Cole, who leaned back in his own seat. "Let's get to business. I need you to find somebody for me."

Luc stared at the man he'd recognize in passing but no more. "I don't think—"

"You don't think with your arm, Saint. You think with your brain, your special ops brain. And that's what I need right now."

Luc bent his head to one shoulder and then the other, trying to reduce the sudden tension in his neck. "I don't follow."

Cole leaned back toward the camera. "There's a woman

who is in danger. She used to be in your army unit. Hank thought you might know her."

Luc frowned. There hadn't been a lot of women in his company, much less his unit. "Yeah? What's her name?"

"Cecilia Garcia," Hank glanced at something beyond Luc, maybe a file or another screen.

"Don't know anyone by that name. I knew a Wright, a Johnson. No Garcia. At least no female Garcia." Luc studied Hank's face for a minute, then continued. "You sure she was in my unit?"

"Thought so, but I do know she was in the part of the sandbox you were in two years ago. She was the communications officer for your unit. May have been a temporary assignment."

Luc had some voids in his memory around that time, thanks to the bomb that he'd encountered in one of the houses he'd visited as a "peacekeeper". "Sorry, man. If it was around the time of my forced retirement, I might not remember her."

"Okay, but I still need your help. You were pretty resourceful when you were in the field. I need that type of skill now." Hank averred.

With a sigh, Luc shook his head. "I'm not one hundred percent, Hank. I don't think I ever will be."

"You working?" Cole interrupted and Luc bit back a curse.

"I'm working as a security guard," he bit out. Nothing more than a night watchman for a car dealership. No weapon, nothing more than a cellphone and a flashlight to hunt with. If he found anything more dangerous than a raccoon going through the garbage, he was supposed to call the cops.

"You happy with that job?" Cole raised an eyebrow

knowingly and Luc didn't bother to cover his curse this time. Hank and Cole both laughed.

"Look, I know you don't want to hear this, but you need to quit feeling sorry for yourself and get back to what you do best. Figuring out what's going on and fixing it."

Luc gestured with his right hand toward the absent left arm. "And this is what I got to show for it."

"No, that's what you got trying to save the world. If you hadn't gone in the house after that kid, you wouldn't have been in it when it collapsed," Hank shot back, his face as impassive as his tone.

Luc was reaching to end the call when Cole interrupted again. "Hear Hank out, Saint. Just a couple minutes. If you still feel like throwing your laptop out the window, fine. But listen."

Luc gritted his teeth but nodded and Hank outlined the issue.

"Cecilia Garcia was in the Army for eight years, went in right after high school. She excelled in her training, rising to the level of Sergeant. Three years ago, she was assigned to your unit as a communications specialist. She went on to other assignments until last year, when she was brought up on charges and court martialed."

Luc stared at the monitor. "Court martialed? For what?"

Hank looked grim, "Drug charges. The records show that she helped in distribution. She didn't get prosecuted, there apparently wasn't enough evidence to bring criminal charges, but she still got dishonorably discharged." Hank glanced away again and gave the exact date of discharge.

"Okay, so what does that have to do with me?"

Cole had been leaning away from the camera while Hank spoke but tilted forward. "Hank and I think you could find her and get her to rethink her plans."

"Me? Go after a drug distributor?" Luc tried to keep his voice calm but when he was a kid, it was all he could do to stay away from the disease and death that scourged his neighborhood. Drugs had been an escape and money-making venture for a number of his classmates and he'd joined the military in part to escape the same future.

"No, to go after a woman who's determined to prove herself innocent. She's going after the people she thinks set her up." Hank said.

"How do you know that and not know where she is?"

"I got a call from one of my guys in the southeastern region. He found out through some of his sources that she's stirring up some stuff down there. Look, Saint. The woman didn't have a smudge on her record until this event occurred. She was found with files on her computer that implicated her in the distribution network for the drug ring but there wasn't any other evidence. Apparently, the court martial was based solely on that. Now, she's on a warpath, not worried about the shit storm she's creating by looking for the guys that set her up."

"I still don't see how I can help," Luc said.

"You have the computer know how to run her down. We don't have the time or personnel to devote to this right now." Hank grunted in irritation. "I don't have a computer specialist on hand that can do this job. Plus, you have the field experience I need in case the situation heads south."

Luc again gestured toward his left side. "I'm not in the same shape I was before."

"So? You keeping up with your shooting? PE?" At Luc's nod, Hank continued. "Then you have the job skills I need. The ones Garcia needs. Now, we gonna sit here and chat or you gonna accept the job?"

Luc stared into his monitor for a second before nodding with a jerk. "I'll give it a shot."

Hank quoted an hourly rate for his time that had Luc spinning for a second, then promised to send a file with the particulars on to Luc. He ended the call with one final jab. "Think of it this way, Saint. You can be the girl's savior with the blessings of your boss, this time."

2

"Damn it!" Celie kept her eyes on the road in front of her as she sped up, eyeing the deserted two lane road. She glanced in the rear-view mirror again. Sure enough, a dark sedan trailed behind her, its lights on bright and edging closer. She punched the gas in her Jeep and flicked her own headlights to bright. No sense in being cautious now.

She'd left the diner at midnight as usual and headed to the small trailer that served as her current stomping ground. She'd only been in Avalon for a little over two months, but she didn't feel safe. Had never really felt secure since she'd left the army.

She kept her gaze on the road ahead of her, aware of the glare from the lights in the rear-view mirror. She cursed and swerved to avoid an opossum in the middle of the road, aware of a silly thought that she hoped the car behind her also saw the pokey animal in time. After a mile or so, the car turned off to the left onto a barely visible gravel road, one of the many in Mississippi, not quite private roads.

She breathed a sigh and shifted in her seat. "If I can last

another week at the diner, I'll have enough." She muttered and mentally calculated the amount of money she'd need for the next step in her solo mission.

She made her own turn onto the gravel road leading to her current home. Two miles down the swamp access road, she turned into her driveway. The trailer, a remnant of the eighties, loomed in the dark, the sparse yard surrounding it short and neat. The mobile home may be ancient, but her landlord kept the structure and attached grounds clean and neat.

She let herself in the house, sighing at the heat that still permeated the aluminum frame and inside, despite the late hour. Summer in the deep south was scorching but she refused to run the window air conditioner when she was at work.

Switching on the ceiling fan in the living room, she leaned over the couch and switched on the living room air cooler. Ignoring the urge to stand in front of the air flow for a few minutes, she instead walked to the bathroom where she shed her jeans and tshirt. Both smelled of grease and fish, the main offerings at the diner. As she strolled back into the living room in her bra and panties, Celie found the huge pickle jar she kept under the sink and dropped the evening's tips into it, toting the amount on the small slip of paper at the top of the pile. As of tonight, she had enough to leave Avalon and head to Jackson. She'd give her boss notice in the morning.

A trill of her cell phone made her jump and she clutched the opaque plastic jar so tight it popped as the side caved in a bit. Replacing the lid, she stuffed it back under the sink, behind the dish detergent, plunger and bucket of cleaning materials. Then she pulled her phone from her small backpack and headed to the bedroom. Once in there, she paused to turn on that room's small air conditioner and, removing her bra, pulled a large tshirt over her head. The army shirt, one a former boyfriend had left at her place years ago, had worn down to a soft, threadbare covering, ideal for the hot summer and fall nights in the south.

A tug from under the mattress revealed her small laptop and with the phone in one hand and the computer in another, Celie started to work. Glancing at the text, she smiled. Another tip and another step toward the man who'd forced her out of the military.

The next morning the phone's alarm woke Celie before dawn and she stumbled into the kitchen to put a pot of coffee on. She'd sacrificed a lot lately, but her coffee, she couldn't give up. She sipped the hot brew cautiously as she tied her running shoes. Her work out clothes, tattered sweatpants, cut off at the thigh and another faded tshirt, this time with the sleeves cut off, were a far cry from the full pack and fatigues she'd worn for PE in the past. Still, they served their purpose. She tucked the house key into a slit in her waistband, alongside a small pen knife and headed out to run.

After her run Celie headed to the back of the trailer, out of sight of the road, where she'd collected an assortment of what most people would call trash or debris. She spent an hour and a half with the tires, wooden bench, and soda bottle weights until she was exhausted and had sweat-wet clothes. She headed inside and the shower. Another day's work, another night spent on the computer. When would she find the one clue that could clear her name?

The small diner hunkered on the side of the road, complete with a partially paved parking lot. Celie found a spot in the back of the building, hopefully with enough shade to keep the temperature in her Jeep in the low hundreds and grabbed her small backpack before heading inside. Her work outfit consisted of jeans and a diner tshirt, which Ernie, the owner, provided each employee. However, if you weren't a medium to extra extra large, you were out of luck. Celie tucked her roomy medium in her jeans and grabbed a sticky pad.

"Can you work some extra, C? Junie is gonna be late again," Ernie called from the kitchen, his hands busy with the mornings offerings of biscuits, gravy and sausage.

"I can for a few hours. How late?"

"Six or six thirty. She has to wait for her mother to get off work to watch her kids. Damn lazy husband can't get off the couch long enough to feed the little buggers." The last part of his reply was grumbled as Ernie bent his head and addressed the immense bowl of dough.

"I can do that. But I need to talk to you later, okay?"

Ernie's head shot up at her request. Celie was good at keeping her head down and doing her job without any complaints. For her to bring attention to herself was something new. "You want a raise or something?"

She shook her head and turned at the sound of the door opening. As she headed to pour a couple of regulars' coffee, she tossed over her shoulder. "Nothing like that. Just a word later."

Later didn't come until the morning crowd dwindled into nothing. After commuters stopped and got breakfast sandwiches to go, fishing buddies stocked up on sandwiches and chips at the counter, and truck drivers filled up their thermoses, Celie wiped down her stations and headed back to start the dishwasher.

She worked alongside Ernie silently until the breakfast mess was cleaned up and then turned. "I need to give you my notice. For one week."

He slumped. "Damnit, Celie. Why you want to do that?"

"I have somewhere I need to go."

"And you can't just go there and come back? I'll give you time off, even pay you for it, if you don't say anything to Junie."

Celie smiled. Junie could have asked the world of Ernie and he'd give it to her. Other than do something for her husband, whom he despised. "I appreciate that, but I don't know how long I'll be gone."

He sighed, "Okay. One week? Maybe Junie's mom will be willing to take over your shift for a little bit. Then I can get some high school kid to work, maybe."

Celie left him muttering and headed to the front of the diner, where she started assembling take out sandwiches. As she worked, she wondered if she'd ever get something other than waitressing.

It was a long way from her job as a communications specialist, something she'd enjoyed and been good at. Making sure lines of communication were open and functioning for her units had been challenging at times but always felt essential and worthwhile. Now, she spent her time elbow deep in cold cuts and dirty plates. "How the mighty have fallen," she murmured.

The day progressed as usual, a few patrons trickled in at lunch, followed by another drag on the hours. Celie contented herself in cleaning, all the while planning her next step. A trip to Jackson Mississippi. Maybe a confrontation; hopefully a clue.

By late afternoon, she was ready to leave Avalon that evening. She'd never been good at waiting, now that she had a deadline in sight, the next week would be interminable.

Two customers wandered in, clearly on their way from

one small town to another. Celie took their orders and had them served with iced tea before the tingling started.

She hadn't heard the door open, hadn't seen the tall dark man enter the diner, but he was seated in a booth near the rear of the restaurant when she turned from pouring the tea. She advanced on him, aware of his gaze on her.

The belly deep awareness of him surprised her. She hadn't felt this type of awareness since leaving the military. Certainly not in the last few months. She pulled the order pad from her pocket and stopped a couple feet from him. "Can I get you something to drink?" She nodded toward the laminated menu tucked between the salt and pepper shakers.

"You got sweet tea?" He had a southern accent tinged with some exposure to other parts of the country, she noted.

"Always," she made herself smile a bit and jotted down the drink. "I'll get you some while you take a look at the menu."

She picked up the pitcher she'd set down near the other couple and retrieved cutlery as well as a glass, which she filled with the syrupy liquid. Ernie believed in as much sugar as liquid in his tea.

"Is the catfish fresh?" The man looked up from the menu and added, "I haven't had fresh in a while."

"We get it in every other day, so pretty fresh." Celie found herself answering honestly instead of the canned response she usually gave. In return he smiled and ordered the large platter. As she turned to deliver the order, he added, "You're Celie Garcia, aren't you?"

She didn't run, she didn't whirl around to confront him, she didn't drop to the floor. She ignored his question and proceeded to the kitchen where she turned in his order, along with the other couple's . When she was finished, she told Ernie she'd be back in a minute and escaped to the bathroom.

What did she do now? No one knew her last name here. She went by Johnson, a common name and one she'd used for three months. And one that no one questioned, especially Ernie, who paid her cash every week.

Did she bolt? Her Jeep had gas, she had some cash in her backpack, but not enough. Damnit, she thought she'd been prepared, but this caught her off guard.

She splashed water on her face and stared in the mirror. Her expression, haunted, flattened into one of neutrality. That was who she had to be right now, someone who faded in the background. With brown eyes, curly brown hair tied back in a low ponytail, and nondescript clothes. No one special.

She returned to the kitchen and dished up salads for one table and cole slaw for the catfish. Then, taking a breath, she delivered them to the tables, starting with the cole slaw and pasted on a smile to let them know she'd be right back.

A couple minutes of delay was all she could muster, delivering the spaghetti dinners to the couple. Then she had to serve the catfish. The platter, enough to feed her for a couple of days, was an armload, filled with potatoes, hush puppies and several large filets. He sat, staring out the window at the tangle of vines and trees lining the parking lot, waiting.

When she lowered the platter onto the table, followed by retrieving bottles of ketchup and tartar sauce, he turned his gaze to her. "Sorry, I didn't mean to scare you."

She stared back at him. "How do you know me?"

He tilted his head, "You got a few minutes?"

She nodded jerkily and after letting Ernie know she'd be

on a break, sat opposite him in the booth, a glass of water in front of her. "So?"

"You didn't try to convince me you aren't Celia Garcia."

"It's Cecilia, actually. And no. What's the point?"

Saint studied the lean woman across the table from him as he took a few minutes to salt, season and sauce his food. He gestured toward his plate and asked, "Want some?"

She grimaced and shook her head.

"You been here long?"

"Long enough not to want fish for the next year or so." She took a sip of her water, more as a measure to calm herself, he thought.

"And you planning on staying for a while?"

She frowned at him. "Look. I don't know you. Why would I confide in you?"

"Because I'm here to help."

Barking a laugh, she shoved her water a few inches away from her and started to rise when Saint spoke again. "I know where Troy is."

Caught in standing, Celie leaned on the table and tried to catch her breath. "You do? Where?"

"Have a seat. We'll talk."

3

Saint eyed the woman across from him. "Take a breath, Celie."

She did so, her color turning slightly rosier than it had been a moment before, when she'd looked like she'd pass out. "Where is he?"

"I'm Luc Benatou, by the way. Or Saint, if you want my Army name." He stuck his hand out, unsure if she'd shake but she gave his hand a firm shake and then withdrew. As he shifted to get more comfortable, he brought his left arm up and caught the look of surprise on her face. She'd not seen his prosthesis? She might have made him feel more "normal" but how'd she lasted this long without better observation skills?

"Hi. Where is Troy?" She didn't bite out the sentence, but it was still short and to the point. Saint wasn't sure he wanted to make this visit that brief. There was something about this woman that intrigued him, beyond the case.

"Can we take this somewhere a little more private?" He might be pushing it a little too soon, but Saint didn't feel comfortable talking in the diner. Not with the open room.

"I can't leave til my relief comes in," Celie glanced at the wall clock, spattered and old. "She should be here in a couple hours."

"Great, while we wait, I'll get to work on this." He picked up his fork.

"No, tell me where Troy is." Her hand shot out and grasped his wrist. The sight of her honeyed skin on his darker hand elicited a current of awareness, surprising him. He pulled away slowly and stabbed a piece of fish. "Like I said. I don't want to talk about it here."

She frowned at him and for a minute, Saint thought she might press the matter, but she stood and, taking her glass with her, stalked toward the kitchen.

He watched as she served the other occupants in the room, greeting entering customers and seating them with quiet efficiency. She didn't chat with them like some servers would, instead she held herself distant from everyone, with the possible exception of the cook, who he heard her bantering with.

He ate slowly, savoring the meal and even having a piece of cake to prolong his visit. Finally, a slightly plump woman with rosy cheeks rushed through the door, her purse hanging from one shoulder and perspiration stains already showing through her diner tshirt. Her apologies and thanks to Celie confirmed that she was in fact the relief Celie had mentioned. Saint gave a silent thanks to the obviously distracted young woman. He'd only been able to track Celie Garcia to her place of business, thanks to a newspaper photo. If she'd not been working, his job of tracking her down might have been a little more difficult.

"Bye, see you tomorrow." Celie pulled a small backpack over her right shoulder and glanced at him. "You ready?"

Saint nodded and threw some bills on the table before

joining her at the front door. The surprised looks the cook and server shot their way made him wonder if Celie had made any friends in this little town.

"Follow me." She started toward a battered Jeep in the rear of the building. Saint had barely gotten into his rented SUV when she shot out of the parking lot. Cursing, he started the car and headed out behind her.

They didn't go to an apartment building, didn't go to a house. Instead, she pulled off the two lane road and parked in a gravel lot alongside a slow moving river. Along the edge of a grassy area several concrete picnic tables and benches rested, old, pockmarked and well used. Saint stopped his car and exited as she approached one and perched on the bench, her back to the trees and river.

He straddled the bench and turned to her. "You've got to stop your search."

She arched a brow at him then snorted a laugh, short and bitter. "Bullshit."

When she started to rise, his hand darted out and caught her wrist. As she attempted to pull away, he continued. "You won't get anything out of Troy Evans. He's in prison and not talking."

Celie sank onto the bench deflated and, for a minute, looking defeated. "In prison?"

Saint nodded, "Has been for eighteen months. On a manslaughter charge."

"Of course." She murmured, her head resting on her hand and her hand cupped lightly over her mouth. She gazed out at the road, quiet but for an occasional truck or car passing them.

Saint kept silent, though he wanted to persuade her to give up her vendetta. It would only result in her getting hurt, or worse. Still he waited until she turned her gaze on him. "How much do you know about Troy?"

"I know he was in the same posting as you, working in communications. I know he was probably the man who planted the files in your system. Files that led you to be court martialed and dishonorably discharged for drug charges. And I know he was the man you've been looking for. The man you want to get revenge on."

Celie's eyes darkened and she stood then, a knife held loosely in one hand. Saint eyed it with some surprise. She was resourceful, that was good.

"Who the hell are you?"

CELIE HELD the knife at her side but with a firm grip. Even with his artificial arm, she'd seen it for what it was now, he was a big son of a bitch and could easily take her down if she wasn't quicker. She stepped back, trying to gauge the best way to get to her Jeep. Damnit, she'd have to go past him. Why'd she sat so far away? Her anxiety and anger grew as he watched her with an amused expression.

"I told you. Luc."

She took a deep breath, trying to quell the urge to jump him. She wanted to pummel the man into taking her seriously. "More," she demanded.

He nodded to the knife. "You don't need that."

"More," she bit out louder.

"Fine. I used to be in the Army too. I got out a couple years ago cause of this." He lifted his left hand. The artificial hand matched his dark skin tone but it was dull, not rich and vibrant. "I was contacted by Hank Patterson to get in touch with you."

"Who the hell is Hank Patterson?"

Saint paused for a minute. "You don't know Hank?"

She shook her head and he continued. "He runs a service out west. Provides body guards. Hires vets." He run his hand over his head then muttered. "And you don't know him."

Celie growled. "Look. I don't know you. I don't know this Hank. And I sure as hell don't need a bodyguard."

"No, you need a reality check." He shot back. "The man in jail right now has survived two murder attempts and it looks like he might end up dead before he faces his second anniversary in the place."

She shook her head. "Good riddance." She hadn't been able to locate Troy Evans but she'd learned a lot along the way. The guy had joined the military as a way of getting more customers for his drug business.

"He might be an SOB, but he still isn't the guy who was ultimately responsible for your discharge."

She frowned, "Then who is?" It'd cut down on a lot of time if she had a name.

Saint bit out a curse. "Look. I'm not going to let you get killed just because you got a mark on your record. Go to college. Get a career. Forget about this."

She flicked the knife closed and shoved it in her rear pocket. "Go to hell." She stalked toward her car only to be halted by his hand on her arm. She shot out a kick but only grazed his leg as he moved out of line of the movement. Saint pulled her to him, wrapping his arms around her and forcing her hands behind her. A horn honked and Celie heard a cat call from a passing car. Great. Now she looked as if she was making out on the side of the road.

"Let go."

"Not until you agree to stop this stupid vendetta."

She spat at him, but he again shifted. She'd gotten his

shirt, though. Celie hadn't resorted to spitting on a man since high school and the thought sent a shaft of resentment through her. "Let me go." She tried to wriggle out of his hold, aware of his arms behind her, the hand holding her wrists.

He looked down at her, his brown eyes intent on her face. "You'll hurt yourself, baby. Stop." His tone wasn't that of a combatant and neither was the heat building between them. Celie looked up at him, her body betraying her by softening as she did.

"I can't quit."

His hold loosened a fraction and she relaxed a bit more, thoughts of getting free fading.

"Why?"

"Because if I quit looking for them, my brother's death will be for nothing."

4

C elie sank on to the battered sofa in her trailer and sighed. The heat, stifling and stagnant as ever, was being slowly replaced by the slightly metallic scent of cool air chugging out of the window air conditioning unit.

She'd pulled herself together and decided that soul wrenching didn't need to be done on the side of a road, then had Saint follow her to her trailer. He hadn't responded to her other than to watch her as she'd calmed, then nodded when she gave him scant directions to the trailer. Now, she watched as he wandered around the small kitchen, pulling out glasses and ice.

He moved with the efficiency she'd come to expect out of fellow military personnel. No movement was wasted but, in him, something else came out, a fluid grace. He was comfortable in his own skin, and with the artificial arm and hand he used. There wasn't any hesitation in his movements, but an extra shoulder curl every now and then gave away his method of effecting movement on his left side.

When he turned she shifted her gaze down to the floor.

He held out a glass of iced water to her and sat in a chair near the couch, his own water in his other hand.

"Thanks," she took a sip, the cold liquid cooling her mouth and throat as it flowed down.

"I figured water was better than beer or tea," he drank from his own and sat the glass on the small table in front of the sofa.

"I don't have either. Just coffee." She shook her head. "Look, I'm sorry I lost it back there."

He held up a hand to stop her. "No need. But I'd like to hear more."

She sighed and turned her head away from him, acutely aware of his gaze. It was as if he could see into her more deeply than she'd want anyone to.

"My brother was two years younger than me. We grew up with a father that served in the military. His father and mother had come to Florida from Cuba and instilled in Dad a sense of responsibility, of the need to give back to our country. Dad spent twenty years in the military and when he came out, returned to Florida. My brother and I grew up hearing stories about the Army, how it had helped Dad become a man, start a career, allow him to travel."

She thought of her father, straight and tall, still lean and strong even after leaving the military. "Being a soldier shaped my Dad and I didn't want anything more when I left high school than to make him proud of me." Tears threatened to fall when she remembered her father's face at the news of her discharge.

Heaving a sigh, she took another sip of her water and continued. "My brother joined up as soon as he graduated too. I'd been in for a couple years by then and we'd email, talk on the phone, whatever when we had time. We didn't get leave together much but we'd see each other a couple times a year. He worked in logistics and enjoyed it, had some time on the ground but mainly in offices, figuring out what went where and how." She smiled. "He said it was like a puzzle only with moving pieces."

Saint sat silently, his drink forgotten and watched Celie's expressive face shift as she recounted her family history. He'd not had siblings, or at least his mother hadn't had any other kids. Who knows what his father had done. But, for Celie Garcia, family meant a lot, obviously.

"When I went to the Middle East the first time, Tony somehow managed a short assignment to match the time I was there." She shuddered. "He thought I'd be happy to see him and I was, but he'd finagled a spot in a unit that saw active duty. I'd seen enough fighting by then that I was thankful both of us didn't have front line duty." She glanced at him and grimaced. "Sorry."

He smiled. "No problem." He'd gotten both thrills and chills out of serving on front lines but he'd also had a short-ened career because of it.

"Anyway, we both made it back to our bases intact and I figured we'd each stay our twenty years, get married, have families, pass on the tradition, you know? Then, a couple years ago, I got a call from my Dad. Tony had gotten killed. It had been a 'tragic accident' that resulted in the single fatal-ity, the report said."

"What happened?" Saint cursed his so-called computer savvy abilities. He'd only researched Celie on the way to see her, not any other member of her family. Her history in the military, her post mates and the court martial had been his main focus in that short time period. His first mistake. Nothing happens in a vacuum.

"He'd been at his post, found some paperwork that caused him to check the schedule of some supplies that were being shipped out. He was crushed by a loader, full of pallets. The operator claimed not to have seen him," she ended bitterly.

Saint thought he saw the connection now but urged her to continue. "The inquest that followed exonerated the operator but when I got discharged, I noticed his name in some of my papers. Turns out, Troy Evans hadn't been meant to be the operator that day. Someone called in and he took over for that one load. And then, after the inquest, he transferred from Logistics to Information and Communications."

Saint bit his tongue to prevent cursing. No wonder she was so intent on finding Evans. "He was the operator?"

She nodded and looked at him intently. "He killed my brother. And I bet the reason is there were drugs in that load Tony was checking."

Saint leaned forward, his elbows on his knees and rested his right hand over his left. "It won't bring him back, you know."

She shook her head. "I do know. But what it might do is help my Dad to sleep through the night. Help me look him in the eye and not be ashamed."

"And if you get killed in your vendetta?"

"Why would I get killed?"

"Because this whole operation was bigger, is bigger than Troy Evans. Why do you think he's been targeted in prison?"

Celie stared at him and then sprang up, "I'm going running."

He rose from his seat and glanced at the window, shaded by faded curtains. "It's a hundred degrees out there."

"So? Wait here." She headed down a hallway and Saint cursed. Not effing likely.

He'd sprinted to his car and retrieved his duffel by the

time she returned to her living room, decked out in cut off sweatpants and a tight fitting sports bra. She carried socks and running shoes. Saint held up his bag and she pointed down the hall. He changed into shorts and a tshirt, tightening the harness on his prosthesis. When he returned to the living room, she was already stretching and ready to run, her dark brown hair pulled back into a curly ponytail.

He threw his duffel back in the car and they started out silently, getting into a rhythm. Saint breathed in the familiar moist air of the southeast, recalling the days he'd done this on the streets of Shreveport, getting ready for his own military career. "You regret joining up?"

She shook her head, her gaze ahead on the dirt trail. "No. I loved what I did. I felt like I was making a difference, even if I wasn't on the front lines."

"We couldn't have done what we did without the teams in communications, supply, the medics." He agreed.

She shot him a look and he felt the assessing glance from his head to his feet. "You were in special unit?"

He nodded, "I loved the whole shooting match. The training, pushing yourself. The missions."

She turned to look forward again. "How'd you get injured?"

"I lived up to my name," he chuckled then continued when she shot him a puzzled look. "I got into trouble sometimes. Nothing major, but my commander usually chewed me out cause I took chances that I shouldn't. I'd see a dog or a cat and rescue them, help out a family, that sort of thing."

"Oh, Saint." She nodded, "You were the do gooder."

"That's what they called me. I didn't do it on purpose, it was just impossible not to do something." He shook his head. "Anyway, the last mission I was on was in a little town that had been bombed out of existence. The houses and mosques that were recognizable were only shells. I followed a scrawny little dog into one of them. A kid about five or six was inside, holding the dog. He started to run away from me and tripped over something. The house went up like someone had stomped on a play house. Next thing I knew, the kid was dead, the dog was dead, and I was pinned under a wall." He held up his left arm. "This was the result."

She didn't commiserate, didn't spout any words of consolation. She just kept running, which suited him fine.

They ran until they met a swamp then turned around and started back. Celie had changed sides of the trail upon turning and he realized she was running on the swamp edge. Habit? An effort to protect? Maybe she had some saint in her as well.

"How do you figure the operation is bigger than just Evans?" Her question was quiet but Saint heard the steel behind it.

"The attempts on his life have been traced to a couple different prison gangs. Both are connected to drug rings in the states. But they're competing gangs, not likely to join forces to bring down a small dealer like him."

"He didn't seem that little, based on my research." Celie panted a bit, the tail end of the run tiring her. "He'd cleared at least half a million that I could trace."

Saint nodded, "He did, but he was still just a link in the chain. And I don't think he had the idea of implicating you."

"And Tony?"

Saint shrugged, "Not sure. Maybe it was his idea. Probably was since it was so blatant."

She stumbled slightly then waved off his outstretched hand, getting back into her rhythm. "So, I need to trace the connection. Find the next link."

"No. you need to let someone higher than you do that."

They swerved off the dirt road and into her yard and Celie slowed to a stop with her hands on her hips. "I'm not stopping."

Saint started to argue with her when a blast shattered the silence.

5

S aint had thrown his body sideways and landed a little hard on Celie, resulting in her loss of breath. She gasped and tried to raise up on her arms only to huff a grunt when he pushed her back into the dirt. "Stay down," he bit out and she felt him shift. The sun glinted off the pistol in his hand and she relaxed a little, letting him take the lead in this new mission.

After he'd surveyed the area around them, Saint shifted off of her and held out his hand. Celie ignored it and stood, her heart dropping. The trailer, the old, worn out metal box she'd lived in for almost six months was now a mass of twisted aluminum and burning wood. "My laptop!" she cried and started to sprint to the fire, only to halt as one pop followed another and deteriorated into rapid small explosions. She dropped to the ground again, pulling Saint down with her. "My gun, ammunition," she muttered.

"How much did you have?"

"Only about forty rounds." She'd meant to replenish the bullets that week. They lay in the sparse grass until the last pop sounded and then stood again, staring at the fire as it consumed the last of her earthly belongings, including her money stash.

"Damn!" She'd not given up before, but now, with no clothes, no gun, and no means of paying for the next stage of her plan, she slumped into desolation.

"You're okay. That's what counts." Saint lay a hand on her back.

"Yeah? Easy for you to say." She sniffed and realized she was about to cry. Damnit, she couldn't cry in front of this man.

"Let's call the fire department and police," he reached into his back pocket then cursed. "My cell phone was in your trailer."

She huffed a laugh. "Guess you weren't so lucky either, huh?"

They watched the fire for several minutes before a siren's wail approached them. Celie recognized the volunteer fire department truck and police car as they pulled alongside the trailer. A rotund officer stepped from his car and, hitching up his pants, strolled over to them. "You live here?"

"I do, did." Celie responded.

The fire volunteers dragged hoses to the trailer and began spraying the now dying fire with water. The police officer removed a pad from his breast pocket with some difficulty, as the tight shirt was damp with sweat. He frowned at Celie. "Why'd you not call the fire department?"

"Our phones were in the trailer." Saint responded. "We couldn't leave the fire, so we figured we'd wait til it calmed down then drive into town and report it."

"Neighbors?"

"I don't have any. I'm the only house on the road," Celie said, stating the obvious.

"Still shoulda reported it," the police officer said. He

looked to the firemen and sighed. "Guess I'll go find out what happened." He looked extremely reluctant to go from hot to Hades, Celie noticed but she trailed after him as he approached the smoldering pile.

The police officer stopped and rested his hand on his holster, tipping his head up to stare at the one section of roof that remained. "As old as this piece of junk was, probably was the gas line or the electrical."

Celie bristled. The trailer wasn't a point of beauty but her landlord had kept it in good shape. "There wasn't any propane or natural gas in the house. And the electrical wiring had been redone before I moved in."

"Who told you that?" The officer said with a sneer.

"My landlord." Celie gave the man's name and the sneer disappeared.

"Well, if he had insurance, he's in the plus column," the officer replied and, after being assured the fire was mostly out, turned and started back to his car.

"That's it?" She stalked after him.

"You got renter's insurance?" he asked.

"No."

"Too bad. We'll let your landlord know about the fire, file a report and that'll be it."

"What about an investigation?"

"With a structure this old? No point. It'd cost more to investigate than it's worth." He took another step before turning and, his expression a bit more conciliatory said, "You got a place to stay?"

"I'll be fine." She said, just wanting him gone.

The fire department finished their work in record time as well and within the hour, Saint and Celie stood in the yard staring at the mess. Celie sighed and headed toward her Jeep.

"You got another set of keys?" Saint trailed her.

She squatted and pulled out the extra key from the wheel well. She stood and gestured to the old car. "My assets."

He laughed and, stunned, she joined him. After a few minutes, she made herself stop before she became hysterical and he leaned against the side of the car. "Where are you going to go now?"

"I guess I'll go to the diner and check in with Ernie. He might give me an advance on my last check." She eyed the wreckage of her home before turning away from it. "Everything I had in there is gone anyway."

"Bank account?"

She shook her head. "Cash, in the trailer." She did have a bank account, but it was in California, where she'd been living before she left the military. She didn't have an identification to obtain it, so the point was moot, at least for now. She took a step toward the Jeep then turned, "Your car keys."

"Also in the trailer." Saint grimaced. "I'll have to contact the rental agency. But I do have one piece of good news."

She arched her brow at him and he grinned. "I have a motel room."

Celie stopped off at the diner and spent far more time explaining to Ernie and Junie about the fire and assuring them she was fine than she'd want. When Junie offered her a bed for the night, Celie automatically rejected the offer then wondered why. She knew Junie a lot better than Saint. But knowing he waited for her outside was something that kept her from unraveling right now and Celie held onto that. With a cash advance from Ernie in her pocket and an assurance a couple days' off of work wouldn't cost her her job, Celie returned to her Jeep.

She found Saint scribbling on the back of a gas receipt, intent on his task. "What's that?"

"I'm making a list for you. Cell phone, clothes, so on."

She took the list and eyed it in the growing dusk, then handed it back to him. "Add liquor."

They stopped off at the Greenwood big box store before heading to the motel. Celie had almost depleted her advance by the time she bought her essentials, a pair of jeans, a tshirt and underwear, as well as the cell phone. She'd beg soap and lotion from the motel clerk to expand her possessions. Finally, she found a cheap backpack, mourning the ever packed survival pack she'd lost. It would take nearly a thousand dollars to replace those items, including her gun.

The motel in Greenwood had a hot shower, a pool and, best of all, a laptop. Celie followed Saint into the small suite and, upon eyeing the computer, threw her bag onto the chair and opened it. "Can I use your laptop?" She drew her finger across the trackpad and woke the computer.

"Depends. This place isn't secure." He moved the bag to the bed and flopped down on the chair, stretching his legs out. "You hungry?"

She shook her head, ignoring the rumble in her stomach and glanced over her shoulder. "What's your password?"

His eyes had been closed but now he opened them and speared her with his dark gaze. "Look, you stink. I stink. We need to regroup here. Let's go get something to eat and then we'll make some plans."

Celie wanted to argue then became aware of her own body and the rank blend of sweat, smoke and desperation that covered her. "Okay, we'll shower first, then plan."

He sent her a smoldering gaze then a smile slowly

spread across his face. "I was thinking you could go first, but I'd be glad to join you."

An unwelcome but delicious heat spread through her and she turned away, hiding what she knew was a hot blush. She huffed and grabbed the bag before fleeing the room.

The stinging shower held her in thrall for several long minutes before she reached for the hotel shampoo and soaps. After emptying the small shampoo bottle with several rounds, her hair finally felt clean and she finished up with a brisk washing before toweling off. As she ripped off the price tags from her new clothes, she tried to figure out what was next. How long would it take to get a new ID? Would her father loan her some cash? Should she even contact her father? And what had caused the explosion and fire?

6

S aint took another sip of his beer as he watched Celie bite into the huge burger. She'd insisted she wasn't hungry until they sat down in the restaurant and the server laid a basket of rolls in front of them. She'd demolished half the bowl before coming up for air then sent him a half smile. When their burgers had arrived, neither had wasted time on small talk, but had tucked in. Now, satisfied, if not replete, Saint sat back and enjoyed the sight before him.

Celie Garcia had more resiliency than he'd seen in a while. She didn't cry or bemoan the fact that the clothes she wore were exactly half of what she owned, nor did she appear to fret over the next step in her life. Had her life as first a military brat then as a member of the military trained her for this? Or was it her personality? Or, he wondered, was she really good at hiding her worries?

"It's a good thing you left part of your stuff in your hotel room." She said after taking a sip of her own beer.

"Yeah. I always carry a go bag, just in case, but I'd dropped everything else off when I came. Except for the phone, I'm good." He frowned at the burn phone he'd picked up at the box store, mourning the loss of all his stored info in the charred one left behind.

"I'll call the police department tomorrow and try to convince them to investigate the fire." She frowned and wadded up her napkin, throwing it on the remains of her meal. Clearly, her appetite had disappeared.

"I don't think it would do any good. Besides, I've given a friend of mine a call. He'll take a look at the site and let us know that he thinks."

Celie glanced up, surprised. "You called someone?"

He nodded. "My old unit buddy is a firemen and investigator. He can take a quick look and tell us if he thinks the fire was naturally occurring or something else."

She narrowed her eyes at him. "You think it was arson, don't you?"

"I think it was a warning."

"How? Why?"

Saint leaned forward. "Look, Celie. I found you through tracing some calls and texts, the inquiries you were making on Troy. If I can find you with no more than that, someone else with equal or better skills and equipment than I have can too."

"You think it was Troy?"

"Hell, no. I think it's the organization that's slowly but surely assassinating Troy Evans in prison. And I think they've figured that you know something about their business, whether you do or not. And now, you're a target."

Celie sat back, stunned at Saint's expression. The easy going, even gentle expressions he'd had when they met could have never graced his face. Instead, he resembled a predator, a man who had one thing on his mind. Violence. She saw the soldier he had once been. Taking a deep breath to calm the sudden tension between them, she said, "Look. We don't even know if the fire was set or not. The electricity may have been faulty, just like that cop said."

Saint's face fell into the amiable mask again and he nodded. "You're right. We'll find out more tomorrow. Now, you want some dessert?"

When she shook her head, he settled up the bill and they headed back to the motel, with one stop at the liquor store where, despite Saint's bark of laughter, she chose a chocolate liquor.

The motel room was cozy and cool upon their arrival. Celie spent a few minutes locating the washer and dryer where she deposited their smoky workout clothes. She'd need the shorts to sleep in and insisted on adding Saint's clothes to the mix. In the interim, she'd sipped on iced chocolate liquor, welcoming the bone melting warmth that suffused her body. She'd also programmed some familiar numbers into her burn phone and checked in with her father, chatting lightly, not telling him of the fire or her resulting homelessness.

When she finally had the clothes, dry and smelling relatively free of smoke, she tromped back to the room where she found Saint lying atop one of the two standard beds, watching television. She chuckled and he turned his eyes from the sports channel to her.

"I bet you had a tough time in the Army, sleeping on their beds." She nodded at his feet, which extended a couple inches past the end of the mattress.

"Nah, I just curled up a little. Hell, by the time I got to an actual bed, I was usually too tired to care." He sat up, his eyes following her as she put her things on the closet rack and his on the desk alongside the tv. "You miss the military?"

"Yes. I liked the regular schedule. I liked my job. I know it wasn't that showy or anything, and it sure isn't the stuff that's shown on advertisements to entice kids to join up. But I have a talent for organization, for figuring out how to streamline things. That came in handy in my job. And, like I said. I felt like getting communications set up and running smoothly, or in the interim, solving a communications problem, made the more immediate and necessary elements of things run more smoothly."

He nodded. "Did you plan on staying in for the long haul?"

She nodded back. "You?"

He shrugged. "I guess. My job was a little more, well, unpredictable. I was good at what I did too, which isn't necessarily a good thing in the scheme of it all. I was good at marksmanship. Good at fighting. Overall, I guess I'd have stayed in as long as they'd let me. Not much use of a fighter in the real world."

His expression must have been more vulnerable than he wanted because Celie frowned. "A lot of ex infantry and so on go into security, police work, that sort of thing."

"And spend the nights listening to all night talk radio or drinking coffee, ruining their stomachs and trying to stay awake." He couldn't hide the bitterness in his tone.

"Sounds like you have some experience in that." She quirked a half smile.

Saint grunted and stood, stretching a kink out of his back. "Yeah. When Hank called about getting in touch with you, I told myself I was doing him a favor. Now, I think he did me one."

He picked up the liquor bottle and, uncapping it, took a sniff. It was an odd blend of alcohol and chocolate. Celie laughed and grabbed one of the glasses off the vanity, plucking off the little cap that covered it and poured a generous portion for him. He sipped it cautiously. "Not bad."

She shook her head. "Don't worry. I won't tell any of your big bad buddies you tried a girly drink."

"Just don't tell them it was this good." He sipped again and turned toward the computer. "Let's get some work done before we turn in."

She eyed the computer cautiously. "I thought you said the computer wasn't secure."

He waggled his head. "It isn't but I can make it so." He opened his laptop and insured his VPN was stable then went online. A few more taps and he was in his own network, private and secure. He glanced at Celie, who looked impressed. "I did have some other skills, you know."

"And you were working as a security guard?"

"No college degree."

"Ah," she nodded. He remembered she'd joined up out of high school as well. Could be they were in the same boat.

Celie went to her new backpack and extracted a spiral bound notebook. Plucking the hotel pen from the desk, she sat down on the carpet and crossed her legs, the notebook resting on them. She closed her eyes and sat silently. Saint thought she might be meditating but she opened them and started scribbling in the notebook. An interminable moment later she halted, tucking the pen behind her ear. A dark curl coiled around the pen as if to hold it in place.

"Okay, here's what I know. After my brother's death, Troy was reassigned out of logistics and into communications. I don't have any info on how that happened. There was a period of time that I couldn't account for, maybe he was retraining or something." She gave the dates for the gap and watched as Saint jotted them on the hotel notepad. "He bounced around bases, Florida, Arizona, Kansas. At least five different postings before he ended up in California with me. He also had some overseas postings, short assignments. We served on the same base, same department but had different schedules, so I never really got to interact with him. Hell, I didn't even know he was the lift operator involved in Tony's death until after I was up for court martial."

Her rancor at this came through. She rose and emptied the last of her drink before washing out the glass and filling it with water then sipped it.

"You didn't have any business with him, no joint assignments?"

She shook her head. "I did find one time where we were both in the Middle East at the same time. I was posted there for a couple weeks, getting some extra sat links up for an operation a special ops team was supposed to do. He was in a different area. I think we may have been on the same flight back to Germany, but I'm not sure." She finished the water and thunked the glass on the vanity. "I had the details in my notes in the trailer. Damn it!"

He turned back to the computer, tapping efficiently. She watched as he used the left prosthesis almost as effectively as he used the right hand. When he glanced over his shoulder and caught her watching he smiled. "Go ahead."

"What?" She bent down and plucked up a piece of lint from the carpet to hide her face.

"You want to know about the arm?"

CELIE SAT on Saint's bed with him seated facing her, his left arm in his lap. His left shoulder was not as wide as his right, but she could see striated muscles there, as well as a ridged scar. He'd surprised them both when, after two more drafts of the liquor, he'd unfastened the shoulder strap and removed his prosthesis. Ten minutes later, Celie knew as much as she'd ever dreamed about muscle twitch, brain-controlled prostheses and rehabilitation. She reached out with a tentative hand to touch the elbow of the apparatus and marveled at the intricacy of the gears and cords that made up the thing. When she lifted her gaze to Saint, his expression gored her.

"What's wrong?"

"Nothing." He turned to rise and she reached out to stop him, her hand glancing over his taut stomach. He'd removed his shirt during the time they'd discussed the arm and his gleaming torso, complete with sparse black chest hair on his upper chest, drew her gaze. Celie admitted to herself she had spent as much time observing this beautiful man as she had listening to his lecture. Her touch elicited a tightening that she could see as his stomach muscles flexed.

"What is it? Did I do something to your arm when I touched it?" She knew she hadn't damaged the mechanism, but something had happened.

"No. I told you, it's nothing." He strode to the bathroom and the door closed behind him with a decisive snick.

She'd washed his glass and returned it to the vanity then retrieved her notebook by the time he opened the door. She stretched her legs out, writing silently for several minutes, eyeing him every now and then as he pounded on the computer. Finally, she threw the book down and stalked over to him. "Tell me what I've done."

He didn't meet her gaze but kept typing. She repeated her demand only to more silence. Finally, she cupped the laptop screen and lowered it to his hands then leaned into him until her face was inches from his. "Tell me."

He turned his head then. His face, his mouth, was so close she could smell mint on his breath. His eyes lowered to her mouth and he muttered, "If you don't want me to kiss you, you better move."

Celie didn't move. She hadn't expected this turn of events but she didn't move. After a breath, he came in for the kiss. His mouth, warm, full and so soft, covered hers with purpose. She leaned into him, her hand cupping his cheek, and returned the kiss in full force. Everything that had happened that day, his appearance, the fire, the knowledge that she might be in danger, faded in significance to this feeling.

She drew away with one small kiss of farewell and whispered. "What did I do?"

He lowered his head and sighed. "Nothing. I have a problem with this." He tilted his head toward his left shoulder.

"Your arm? Why?"

When he raised his head to meet her gaze his face held wonder. "You don't care?"

"That you lost your arm? Yeah, because it hurt you. That you have an artificial arm? No. You need it, you use it beautifully; it serves a purpose."

He stood, making her take a step back. His arms came around her in a hug and he pulled her close into him. Their kiss had affected him as well. His erection pressed against her and Celie wondered if the night might bring more than she had planned.

Instead of extending the initial kiss and embrace, he stepped back and ran a hand over her hair and the strands loosened from her ponytail. "You are something else, Celie Garcia."

How did she respond to that?

He turned and motioned to the computer. "I've put out inquiries about the things we talked about. It might take a couple hours or more to get responses." At her nod of acceptance, he continued. "We might as well get some rest in the meantime."

Celie nodded again and turned to retrieve the sweat shorts. After brushing her teeth and washing her face, she came from the bathroom to find him in the bed, his prosthesis removed once again and hooked up to a pack on the table. Celie put her used clothes, folded neatly, on the luggage rack and turned down the covers of the other bed. She slid in between the sheets and sighed, realizing how tired she really was. When she turned on her side, she saw Saint had done the same and he was watching her.

"Thanks for helping me out, Saint."

"You're welcome, Celie." His voice, already low and rich, had deepened further.

"Good night," she said as she reached for the bedside switch. He murmured his response and the room became dark, with only the lights of the parking lot seeping in through the sides of the closed curtains. Celie fell asleep to the sound of his breathing and the slow hiss of the air conditioning.

7

Celie was doing pushups when Saint opened his eyes the next morning. He watched a couple minutes as she silently continued, though he knew she was aware of him. He rolled over and sat up, his hand rubbing across his face in an effort to force wakefulness, then stumbled to the bathroom.

The hotel coffee maker was half full and he gratefully filled a Styrofoam cup with the dark brew and took a sip. The stuff didn't resemble coffee but he hoped it had enough caffeine to do the job of jumpstarting his neurons. The shower sure as hell hadn't.

Celie hopped to her feet and smiled at him, her face bright and slightly flushed from her exercise. "Good morning."

"Morning," he mumbled and crossed to his rumpled bed and sat on the end.

She shook her head at him. "Not a morning person?"

"Hell no."

"Okay," she drawled and went in search of her shower things.

By the time she exited the bathroom, dressed and her face shining, he'd drank another cup of the awful stuff the motel called coffee and was able to be civil. "Good morning, Celie." He tried again.

She chuckled. "How'd you fare in the military, not being alert in the morning?"

"All I had to do was move. Listen, watch and move. I can do that. Just not think or communicate for a few minutes." He waggled his head. "I'm better than I was when I was a kid. My mom had to get me out of bed by tilting the mattress sometimes."

She laughed with him and motioned toward the computer. "Can we check and see if there was an answer to your questions?"

"Not without a decent cup of coffee and some breakfast. I'll even settle for fast food," he countered. When he thought she'd argue, he added, "I think I might have a plan."

They went next door to a fast food restaurant and indulged in pancakes, as well as breakfast sandwiches, in his case. A large coffee that actually resembled the real thing made his morning much more bearable and Saint followed Celie back to the motel room with the added wakeup call from her toned back and rear.

The laptop yielded answers to the blank dates and assignments Troy Evans had completed in the Middle East. In addition, Saint found information that added to the dread already swelling in his stomach as he read the reports. Sleeplessness and worry had pulled him out of bed in the early hours and resulted in more information on her brother's death, as well as Troy Evan's civilian life before the military. Now, as they reviewed his assignments in the states and overseas, Saint started putting things together.

"You got your notebook?" He asked. She pulled it out

and held it to him. "No, you can write it down. But here's what I've found out." He turned in the desk chair and motioned for her to have a seat. She folded her legs into a crossed position on the bed and opened the pad. "I looked up your brother's death last night—"

"You did? When?"

He waved a dismissive hand. "I couldn't sleep and got up for a couple hours. Anyway, he had made a comment in some of the paperwork that there was some discrepancy in weight of pallets. The pallets were supposed to have the same things on them, same weight, same everything, but in three shipments to the Middle East, there were three pallets that were lighter by a few pounds. Evidently, not enough to cause the pallets to be pulled and inspected. Everything else, including random inspections, had cleared."

Celie flicked the pen back and forth between her fingers. "You think that was the connection for Tony and Troy?"

Saint nodded. "Troy was stationed there too. He had another job, storage. Tony had the job of final inspection and shipment, insuring the distribution and so on."

"So, if Troy wanted to send some drugs to someone on a base, he could easily have planted them in a pallet. It was the perfect job for that." She jotted down some notes then glanced back at him. "Anything else?"

He nodded grimly. "I think this is a lot bigger than you and I can handle."

Celie's flicking stopped and she dropped her hand to rest in her lap. "What do you mean?"

"I don't think Troy was much more than a lower middle-man. If I'm right, there's a huge distribution network going on here. One that might encompass a lot more than just one guy."

"Did you find more information?" She leaned forward,

eager to see the data.

"Not really. But Hank has a guy, Tank, who works in Georgia. Interesting guy. Anyway, he has mad hacking skills, way better than mine. He was one of the emails I got this morning." Celie stood from her position at the end of her now made bed and joined him at the laptop. He'd pulled up the email. "I sent some requests to Hank and he forwarded them to the necessary people. That man has more connections than any human should have. Anyway, Tank got into some federal files and found a thread."

Celie's read through the email and frowned. "There's no one mentioned there."

"No, but the DEA has been trying to find a connection between Troy Evans and a wider distribution affecting the whole armed forces." Saint watched her as the weight of that information sank in. "Now you know. It's not going to be easy, Celie. May be impossible to connect anyone other than Evans to your brother's death and your court martial."

She took a deep breath, trying to quell the urge to move, to do something, anything. "But I still have to try."

"No. *We* have to try."

They ran errands that morning. Celie replaced her pistol and ammunition with little effort through a private sale. Saint's supply in the motel room impressed her, with more pistols, a rifle and a couple of wicked looking knives she was sure he could wield effectively.

They checked out of the Greenwood motel and drove the eighty or so miles to Jackson. There, Saint insisted on more supplies, despite her protest, replying that he'd be reimbursed for expenses including supplying them both with tactical packs and body protective gear. By the time he was finished, Celie felt as if she were back in the Army and ready for a frontline assignment and, maybe, she was.

"I want to see Troy." Celie cut into the baked potato as she made the statement, ignoring Saint's pause as he loaded his fork with his own steak and grilled vegetables.

"It might take some time to get permission. He's been in solitary for a bit."

"When did you find that out?"

"This morning. Hank's source found out he's been there for being involved in a knifing. Nice guy, apparently."

Celie stared at the food in front of her, her appetite waning. Saint tapped the edge of her plate with his knife. "Eat. You'll need the energy."

She nodded and automatically speared a piece of meat, chewing on it without tasting. "Can Hank pull more strings?"

"We'll find out." Saint pulled his phone from his pocket and texted his boss, then set the phone down on the table beside him. They ate in silence for a minute before the phone trilled. Giving Celie a wry smile, Saint answered.

"Hey, boss," he drawled.

"What the hell you doing? I wanted you to get Garcia out of the line of fire, not toss her in the inferno."

"She's already in, boss. Her trailer was destroyed yesterday and, odds are, it was deliberate." He mouthed sorry to Celie who frowned at him and laid her fork down. He hadn't shared that piece of news with her yet.

"Explain," Hank barked.

"There was an explosion and fire, destroyed the structure. I had a friend look into it, since the place was old and the local cops didn't seem inclined, nor did the property owner. My guy found evidence of an accelerant that shouldn't have been there."

"Well, hell." Hank muttered. "What info do you think

you can get out of Evans if you do see him? I'll have to call in a lot of favors to get this done."

"Hold on." Saint held the phone out to Celie. "He wants to talk to you."

Celie wiped her hands with a napkin and accepted the phone. "Hello?"

Saint watched as she introduced herself and then waited. When she sent him an imploring gaze he knew she'd been asked the question.

"I want to know why he planted the files in my computer. What, if any connection that had with my brother's death. Who is responsible for blowing up my home."

She was silent then added, "I'm sorry if it's a hassle getting us into the prison to see him, Mr. Patterson. It was a hassle when I had to find a job with a dishonorable discharge. It's been a hassle facing my father every time I visit him and know he won't see my brother again. And it sure as hell was a hassle to have everything I own blown to bits yesterday."

She punched the end button and all but threw the phone at Saint. He caught it in time for it to trill. He didn't answer it but held it out to her again.

"What?" She barked. Saint had to give it to her, she didn't intimidate easily.

"I see. Thank you." Celie handed the phone to Saint and returned her attention to her food, clearly in a better mood than a minute before. He gingerly held the phone to his ear. "Yeah?"

"She's a tiger," Hank drawled.

"That she is." Saint smiled. Or maybe a jaguar, but equally as dangerous when cornered.

"I'll have a plane for you by this afternoon. I assume you wouldn't clear security?"

"Nope." Saint thought of the go kits he'd assembled earlier, brimming with items that would never make it through a security check.

"Okay. Let me see what I can do. I'll call you back."

Saint ended the call and leaned back, watching Celie finish off her meal. "Want some dessert? We've got some time."

They spent the afternoon at a shooting range, which helped assure Saint that, even though she'd been out of the military for a bit, Celie had kept up with her marksmanship. That, with her workout routine might even put her in better shape than him.

"You said you think the operation is bigger than we thought, right?" Celie asked quietly as they stored their pistols and prepared to leave.

"Yeah, I just don't have enough information to prove it."

"All the more reason to talk to Troy," She leaned against the high counter in the indoor range. "If we can question him, we might find out who his boss is."

"And do what?" Saint plucked her backpack and his bag and, with a hand on her back, ushered her out of the building and into the bright sunshine.

She didn't respond until they were in her Jeep and on the interstate headed toward another motel and an afternoon of waiting. "I guess I'll have to turn it over to the DEA."

Celie didn't mention that before turning anyone in, she wanted to confront them first.

The Jackson hotel had a lot more amenities than the one in Greenwood and Celie delighted in using the inside pool to swim laps while waiting for Hank's call. If she got some looks from the other patrons for her swimming outfit of a sports bra and cut offs, too bad. She already owed Saint or Hank more money than she wanted to think about.

Saint suggested they order room service while waiting for the phone call but Celie couldn't wrap her head around this in mid day. Instead, they ordered a pizza and sodas and whiled away the afternoon working out in the gym, watching mediocre afternoon television and playing poker with a deck of cards Celie unearthed from her Jeep's glove compartment. Saint finally threw his hand in, accepting the fact that he was a worse poker player than Celie and suggested dinner.

"I thought you wanted to stay in for more privacy with the call." Celie said, though she jumped up and grabbed a brush, ready to get out of the room for a while. Though neither acknowledged it, there was a thrum of awareness between her and Saint that had been growing ever since their kiss. Fresh, or stagnant, in Jackson's case, air might relieve the tension between them.

"I did but this is taking longer than I expected. We might as well go get something to eat and get some more planning done afterward."

She dashed into the bathroom and washed off, changing into the last clean outfit she had. She'd swam in the shorts, worked out in still another pair she'd purchased to sleep in and now tore off yet another price tag and dressed in still more jeans and tshirt. After brushing her hair and teeth and applying some lip gloss, she exited the bathroom. Saint took his turn and they were soon outside. Saint pointed out a chain restaurant across the interstate that served a blend of Tex Mex and Americana food. "That okay with you?"

She nodded and soon they were seated with chips and salsa before them and beers on the way. Fajitas and queso had a powerful effect on her mood, she realized and found herself laughing and chatting with Saint as if it were a date rather than a mission.

How was that? Saint lounged in the booth opposite her, alternately swirling a chip in the mixture he'd concocted out of queso and hot salsa and delving into the steak fajita. He'd spent the time they ate telling her of his misfortunes as a kid and teenager, being taller and ganglier than other kids, "but not talented in any sports they wanted to play". Instead, he relished track and field, medaling in his state's cross country events in his senior year. "When I figured out I wanted to go into the Army, I found out running had put me a little ahead of the game."

Celie chuffed a laugh. "I'd say so. Even though my dad was in the Army, I didn't do much sports other than cheer-leading. Tumbling and flying isn't something that translates well into Army PE."

"Flying?" Saint quirked a grin at her. "You been hiding a talent?"

She took a sip of her beer, the second one of the night. "It's the term used for when the male cheer team members toss girls up in the air. I was a flyer since I was a little shorter than the other girls, and skinnier." She shrugged. "Not much of a talent."

"But it must take guts to trust your team mates enough to let them throw you about."

"Oh, I didn't necessarily trust them. I threatened them with my dad. He's big, like you." She grinned when he laughed.

"You work out a lot now. Is that a holdover from the military?"

"A little, but I've always been active. High school was cheering, like I said. Then when I joined the Army I spent a lot of time after basic in training. Inside training, learning electronics, computer programs and so on. It was hard, you know? Sitting inside for so many hours when I'd expected to be out and active. So, when I got out of the classroom, I found ways to use the energy that pent up during the day. Swimming, running, weight training. It helps with all the extra energy I have."

They talked through the rest of the meal and refused dessert before heading back out to the Jeep. When Celie asked if he wanted to drive, Saint looked surprised. She held out the keys, "I had two beers to your one and I'm feeling that last one. Do you mind?"

He accepted the keys and headed back to the hotel room. Celie sat in a relaxed heap, her head back against the headrest as she watched the dusk settle on the city streets. When her window glass shattered, she startled upright only to be shoved into the floorboard. Saint shook her shoulder. "You hit?"

His voice brought her back to sudden clarity and she inventoried her body's functions and any pain. "Some glass cut my arm, that's it. What happened?"

He kept his eyes on the road. Celie tried to sit as wide as possible in the tiny floor space, bracing herself as he swerved from lane to lane. "What are you doing? You want to get us arrested?"

His tone was grim when he responded, "Hell no, not in this city. But we need to get clear of the hotel, at least for the night."

"What about our things?" She didn't want to face purchasing another round of essentials. And the computer. "Saint, we have to go back. We left the laptop and notes there."

He cursed and swerved again, then reduced speed. "Okay, we'll go back and get that stuff." His driving was controlled but the expression on his face reminded Celie he'd been a special forces operator. Maybe still was.

They wheeled into the parking lot and Saint hustled Celie out of the car. A shower of safety glass chunks exited the Wrangler with her and she wondered how bad she looked. Instead of going toward the front entrance, however, Saint steered her to a side entrance where he swiped the room card on the locked door. They raced to the third floor via the stairs and, once he determined the hallway was clear, Saint allowed Celie to follow him to the room.

Once there they made quick work of packing up. Celie glanced at the vanity mirror and swore then swiped a hand towel and wet a washcloth before stuffing both into a trash can liner. She paused and grabbed her stack of clothes and pushed them in her backpack, wet swim clothes included.

Five minutes later, both of them were in the Jeep again, after Saint swiped most of the glass out of the seat and floorboard with his left hand. Once they were on the road, Celie stared forward, her mind racing. "Who's trying to kill me? And how'd they know we were in Jackson?"

Saint concentrated on his driving for a few minutes then took an exit toward Jackson airport. "What'd you bring with you from the trailer?"

"Nothing. The Jeep. I didn't recover anything, remember?"

"And no one knew we were coming to Jackson." He murmured then cursed. "Someone must have put a tracker on your car. It's the only way they'd be able to find you."

The airport loomed ahead and Celie's thoughts raced. "What are you doing? We can't go anywhere til Hank calls."

"We need to get rid of this car. We'll get a rental."

"And then?"

He glanced into the rear view mirror.

"Then we're getting the hell outa Jackson."

8

S aint scrambled to think of the next step. He'd not been the one with the plan since he'd been in the military and found his skills had atrophied in the past year or so. Time to exercise them, as he had his body.

Once they'd stored the Jeep in the long term parking and hiked to the car rental, he'd come up with a tentative plan. After asking and finding out that being shot at was a sure fire way to sober up, Saint directed Celie to drive. "Get on the interstate going northwest."

"Where are we going?"

"Hopefully somewhere no one will be able to locate us for a couple days. We need to regroup and make a plan that isn't on the fly."

They drove into the western sun and then dark for hours. Saint relieved Celie on the last leg of the journey and when they crossed into Louisiana Celie shot him a surprised look. "We're leaving Mississippi?"

"You attached?"

She laughed ruefully, "No. Just surprised."

"Hey, if we get a chance to see Evans, we'll be flying to

Kansas so the only thing that matters is that we're relatively close to an airport."

She sat quietly for a few minutes then continued, "What did you mean we need to make plans that aren't on the fly?"

"We've been reactive, Celie. Ever since your trailer got blown to bits, we've been looking over our shoulders and scrambling to keep up. Now, if you're going to get your answers and stay alive, we need to come up with a decent plan of action."

"I have a plan." She sounded offended and Saint hid a grin.

"Okay, lay it out for me."

Her silence provided the answer he looked for. "Look. I'm with you in finding out who is gunning for you and to find out about Tony's death as well. But we're up against an unknown and just being a step ahead isn't enough, clearly. Let's get somewhere we can both feel at ease and rest and, hopefully, we'll get some better info on who is after you."

"Could be you they're targeting," she muttered.

"Maybe, but the last person I pissed off was a bartender in Shreveport when I spilled a beer on him, and I left a tip big enough to settle him down."

She slouched down in the seat and put her knees up against the glove compartment. "Fine. Let's go to the swamps and plan."

CELIE GOT out of the SUV and stared around her. The state park cabin Saint had procured was small but looked decent from the outside, with a small porch and even what looked like a couple of rocking chairs. Beyond it, midst the shadows cast by trees and bushes, ran a slow current of a swamp. She felt eyes on her, but not the eyes of two legged predators. "I didn't think you would take me seriously."

Saint, busy retrieving their things from the hatch replied. "It's out of the way. Private."

She glanced around her, looking for lights, people. "That's for sure."

Once inside the slightly damp feeling cabin, she flicked on lights and surveyed their new retreat. The small building hosted a living space, complete with sofa and easy chair with the requisite television attached to the wall. A kitchenette ran the length of one wall. Two doors opened off the living area, one to a bathroom and the other to a bedroom. Celie followed Saint to the doorway and spied one bed. She wheeled around, ignoring the thrill of heat in her lower body. Finally, she settled on the kitchen.

"You covered everything except one, Saint."

"What?" He stood at the doorway, rubbing his left shoulder.

"We don't have any food."

Two hours later, Saint sat with a cup of coffee and a soggy sub sandwich in front of him. He forced down the food, wondering how long it had been sitting in the cooler. Celie had picked at the sandwich, not even pretending to eat. "Sorry. The gas station didn't have much in the way of food."

"Don't worry about it." Her tone didn't assure him.

"At least we have coffee." He sipped his.

"Thank God," she muttered and took a gulp of her own black brew. Finally, after several minutes, she stood and dumped the uneaten food into the trash can and filled her cup from the carafe. "Plans?"

"Plans," he gratefully dumped his food as well and

plucked a bag of tortilla chips off the counter, bringing it to the table. He retrieved his computer and while it was booting up, checked the cell phone for messages. "Hey, we got a message from Tank."

She perked up at that. "When? What does he say?"

Saint typed in a reply and waited. "He sent me an email with some information in it. On Troy and his past activities, as well as some in the military. Looks like Troy was a busy boy."

Celie flopped into the seat across from him. "We know that."

"No, more than we've figured in the past. Hang on." He tapped at the computer and pulled up his email. Opening the file, he motioned her over to sit beside him. They read silently for a while and Saint whistled. "He's the poster child of what not to do as a teenager."

Celie shook her head. "How'd he even get in the Army with that record?"

"Juvenile." Saint said. "I wish I had a printer. We could use one to record the names we need to look up."

Celie stood and went into the bedroom, returning with her notebook and pen. "Give me names. I'll write them down and then we can look them up from there."

They spent several minutes going through Troy Evans' criminal history, deciding what petty crimes were unnecessary to investigate and which names were more interesting. As they worked, Saint sent an idle thanks to whomever ran the whole works that he'd chosen a better path for himself as a kid. Troy had made mistake after mistake as a teenager, had ended up in juvie time and again and had accumulated enough experience in petty crimes and possession to serve as a training ground for his future drug distribution career.

Finally, Celie leaned back and surveyed the list of

names they'd accumulated. As she did, Saint closed the email and reviewed the rest, deleting ads for male enhancement, workout supplements and so on. He glanced over at her to find her frowning. "Do you recognize any of the names?"

She shook her head then looked up at him. "No, but I didn't think I would."

His inquiring gaze prompted her to continue. "I knew there were drugs in the army. There are everywhere. But I didn't hang around with anyone who used them, as far as I know. And I made a point of steering clear of anyone who had even a shadow of selling the stuff. And as far as I know, neither did my brother."

"He was in a job that might have put him in a bad position, Celie." At her sharp look, he continued. "I don't mean using or getting involved. I mean he was in logistics, which is too close to supply. Too close to seeing something going on. Which he did, eventually."

Her lips thinned, "Right." She glanced at the names again then tapped her pen against the paper. "What if someone finds out we're looking into Troy's associates, Saint?"

He huffed a sharp laugh then gestured around them. "Too late. We wouldn't be here if they already didn't suspect."

She shrugged and stood then stretched. As she did, a thin line of skin showed between the line of her shorts and top. Saint couldn't look away from the golden skin it revealed, couldn't ignore the spurt of heat running through him. Her closeness, the slight scent of fresh, lightly scented skin rammed home the knowledge of that one bed in the other room.

He swiveled away from her in his chair then stood. "I'm

getting a cup of coffee then going to the couch. If we're gonna spend the night online, I'm getting comfortable."

He took the couch over, intentionally using as much of the furniture as possible. He couldn't get distracted by her, wouldn't do it. Distraction right now could mean her getting injured or worse, if he wasn't alert.

She sat in the chair adjacent to him, alternately calling out names, jotting down notes and flicking the pen in her hand. After a few minutes, she swung her legs over one chair arm and started bobbing her foot, up and down, up and down. Then she'd waggle one to the side, back and forth, back and forth. Finally, at the end of his tether, Saint shoved the laptop to the side and stood, "I'm taking a break."

Celie looked up, startled, from the notebook. "Now? We're finally making some headway. This Randy guy, he was in the Army when Troy first joined up. We might find a –"

"Yeah. I know but I need a few minutes." He started toward the door only to stop when she called to him.

"Saint."

"Yeah?" He didn't turn toward her and Celie thought she saw his shoulders tense.

"You know the animals have control out there at night, right?"

"Damn," he lowered his head, then raised it again. "I'm just going to the porch. I'll be back in a few minutes."

Celie shook her head at him. The mosquitoes had as much power out there as an alligator and were as ferocious. She stood and took their coffee cups to the sink where she rinsed them, as well as the coffee carafe. She started to make another pot then put the can of coffee back in the small cabinet. Her stomach already felt queasy from the three cups she'd had so far. Instead, she located a pitcher in the cabinet and filled it with ice, then water. Better.

By the time she'd filled a glass and returned to the chair, Saint was inside, rubbing his neck with his hand. "Bites?" She murmured and bit back a grin at his dark look.

She watched as he stalked to the bathroom where she heard running water and odd sounds, as if he were looking for something. "There's a small bottle of mouthwash in my backpack." She called. "In the front pocket. It'll help a little."

He stomped from the bathroom into the bedroom and returned with a small bottle clutched in his large hand. He opened it and poured a scant amount in his hand then ran it around his neck. Capping it, he stalked to the couch and set it on the small table in front of the couch.

"Better?" Celie asked mildly, her eyes on the notepad.

He grunted and rubbed his neck again, then lower, reaching for his back. He pulled the computer back to him and started tapping. They worked silently for a few minutes then he thrust the computer away from him, setting it on the table. "Damn it!"

Celie watched as he pulled his tshirt over his head with one hand and reached for his back, first over his head and then tried to bend his right arm to the side. His tortured expression told her he'd gotten more than just a couple bites.

She laid her notepad down on the table and rose then walked over to the kitchen area. She rummaged in the cabinets, locating left over coffee creamer, packets of sugar and pepper and an opened box of baking soda. She poured some into a coffee mug and approached the couch. "Move over," she said and nudged his sprawled leg with her knee. When he did she sat beside him and motioned with her hand for him to turn away from him.

His back had several welts rising on it, from the top all the way to his waist line. "Give me the mouthwash," she murmured as she eyed the v shaped expanse before her. His skin was smooth and perfect, beyond the few welts and the scars that cupped his left shoulder. She wanted to run her hands over the entire surface, learning the feel of him. Instead, she accepted the bottle and uncapped it, poured and mixed some in the baking soda, then started dabbing it on his bites. After a minute or two she heard a sigh. "Is it helping?"

"Yeah, thanks," he muttered and then turned his head toward her.

Her hand rested on the last bite she'd treated, the one nearest his waist. There was a small gap where his jeans met the center of his back. His back, bisected by his spine, sported a nicely defined dip all the way down. She glanced down at her hand, tanned and sure, on his darker skin and felt a twinge of need deep inside her. She raised her gaze to him.

As he stared at her, his eyes steady and with maybe a slight question in them, she slid her hand from his bite to the small gap and let her finger dip into the waist band of his jeans. Skin warmed from his body met her fingertips and she ran her hand in a shallow curve to the top of his pants. "I think I got them all," she whispered and removed her hand.

Saint turned to face her, taking the proffered mug then the bottle and capped it, his eyes not leaving hers. "Thanks."

She should stand up, should walk over to the chair and get back to work, her brain told her. But her legs wouldn't follow the command, wouldn't follow the instructions. Instead, she sat there, looking at his face, his lips, his eyes. Eyes full of heat, desire. For her.

When he dropped his head and covered her lips with his, Celie almost sighed in relief. She'd wanted this since their first kiss. Wanted to see if it was as good as she'd remembered. As she lifted her hands to his shoulders and opened her mouth under his, she vaguely marveled, it was even better.

He didn't push her down, didn't take over but somehow, they ended up lying full length on the couch, her under him. Celie explored his back and shoulders, ran her hands over his closely shorn hair and chin, cupped his jaw. How long they spent kissing, cuddling and learning the texture of each other's skin, she didn't know, didn't care. It wasn't long enough. When his hand slid between their bodies and cupped her breast over her tshirt she murmured encouragement.

The shirts came off first, tossed over the back of the sofa, followed by her insubstantial bra. Saint leaned on his left elbow and Celie felt the metal and plastic of his prosthesis cooling her hot skin as it brushed against her side. Even that was sensuous. When he cupped her breast again, his eyes on his hand, she murmured, "I'm little."

He glanced at her with a smile, "But fierce," then his head drooped and his lips covered her nipple. She arched into him, relishing the hot heat as he kissed, nipped and gently suckled at her. When he left one breast to spend equal time on the other, she sighed.

Soon, it wasn't enough. Celie fumbled at his waistband, clumsy in her haste. When he covered her hand with his, she stared at him.

"I don't have any condoms," his frustration was clear and she smothered a groan of her own. "So, we can't."

"No. Not tonight. But tomorrow, I'll find someplace." His forehead came to rest on hers and he kissed her, a short, intense peck. "And when I do, I'll buy a value pack."

She couldn't laugh, not now, but she did smile at him

and nod. He retreated to the bathroom and Celie found her shirt and bra and donned it regretfully.

They sat back in their respective places and took up their tools. Celie sat, her legs bent at the knees and feet on the floor and tried to calm her body. If she wasn't sure it'd result in the same outcome, she'd take a trip outside.

"Okay," Saint sighed. "Let's look into this guy you were talking about. Randy. What was his last name?"

"Fortner." Celie turned a sheet back in her notebook. "He was in Supply when Troy joined. I don't know if they ever connected."

Saint pecked on the computer and cursed, then reached for his phone. A few taps later, "Hey, Tank. I need your help. Yeah?" He glanced at his watch, "Sorry. So, you're up. I need you to hack into some military records for me."

Saint pushed a button and laid the phone on the table, then returned his attention to the laptop. The voice that boomed over the phone was deeper than Saint's and majorly pissed.

"Hell yeah, I'm awake at two o'clock in the goddamn morning. Cause you called me. Hold on." A rustle followed by another, milder curse then he came back on the phone. "Okay. What do you need?"

"I have a Randy Fortner in the Army around the same time as our primary guy. I need to know if they were in the same unit. Had any crossovers."

When prompted, Saint filled in the dates.

"Where'd you come up with this name?"

"It was in the file you sent. He was buried in some other details, but we figured it was worth a try, to see if he's connected." Celie offered.

"Who's that?" The voice altered, became deeper, if possible

"Celie Garcia."

"You the gal that needed some help?"

Celie hesitated and Saint filled in, "She's the woman Hank had me contact, yeah."

"Gotcha. Okay, let's see what we got." Tank rattled off dates, units and companies as Celie tried to jot down everything. When she asked him to repeat the data he offered to send the info in an email. Saint shook his head, "No, we don't want any more traceable records than we have already. Just repeat the info, Tank,"

There was a short pause then Tank complied and Celie nodded at Saint to indicate she'd gotten it.

"What's going on, Luc? You in some trouble?"

"No. We're just gathering data, bud. That's all." Saint's tone held reassurance and Celie hoped the other guy didn't pick up on the tension running through him as she did.

"Okay," the word was drawn out and she knew Tank had gotten the message. "Let me know if I can do anything else. Only not in the freaking middle of the night, okay?"

Saint chuckled and they disconnected. He and Celie looked at each other. She sent him a rueful smile. "I think we may have a connection."

He nodded and started punching in another phone number.

"Saint," when he looked up at her, she continued. "It's late. Let's finish up in the morning, okay?"

He glanced at his watch again and pushed the end button on his phone, then opened up another app. "I'm sending Hank a message. We need some criminal searches on Fortner we can't do."

"And Tank?"

"I don't want him to do them. He's too curious right now

and I don't need to pull him into the mess. His wife is expecting their first kid."

She waited until he was finished with his text then closed the notebook and placed her hand on top of it. "We may have made the connection, right?"

He nodded and closed the computer then leaned forward with his elbows resting on his knees. "I think so. If we can get in to see Evans, we might find out some more."

And then, Celie thought, she'd be able to face her brother's killer.

9

Troy Evans was a little man, skinny and pale from his time spent in solitary confinement. Saint sat across from him and stared through the spotty glass divider separating Evans from them. Celie sat beside him, her body tight and quiet though he could feel the tension vibrating from her.

"Troy Evans?"

"Yeah," the guy muttered his reply, his eyes moving between them as fast as he could swivel them in their sockets. The fact that they were there, without an attorney breathing down their necks, still amazed Saint. Hank had definitely pulled some strings.

"Does the name Tony Garcia ring a bell?" Celie's voice came through solid and steely and Saint watched Evans' eyes dilate.

"No. Should it?"

Celie leaned forward until her face was inches from the divider. "You used a forklift to kill him two years ago."

A sneer erupted from Evan's smooth pale face. "I didn't see him, didn't you read the report?"

"I read it. I just didn't believe it."

"So? That's your problem, not mine." Evans leaned back in his chair. "Still, you want to talk about it, I'm good with that. First time I've been out of that hole in weeks."

Saint watched as Celie's jaw clenched. It was time he added his bit. "Tony Garcia found some inconsistencies in the supplies you were overseeing."

"Inconsistencies, huh? Happens all the time," Evans smirked.

"Yeah, but these happened three times, over three months. All within your responsibility." Saint drawled his reply, not letting the bastard know he was getting riled at him.

"I wasn't a very good counter," Evans shook his head in a mocking mournful manner.

"Oh, these weren't counting errors," Celie mentioned. "They were weight errors. The kind of errors that go by when they are isolated. But if they happen often enough, may end up being investigated."

"I wouldn't know but nobody investigated anything," Evans replied.

"Oh, I know it didn't get investigated. Because Garcia didn't have a chance to report it. He died before he could."

"Too bad. I bet he'd a got a commendation for it, or something."

When Evans smirked again, Saint knew what their means of controlling him was. There was a small tremor at the edge of the guy's mouth, a look in his eyes that told Saint he wasn't as calm as he appeared.

"Yeah. Too bad." Saint ignored the glare Celie sent his way and continued. "But you see, my partner and I are investigating that death, along with some other discrepancies that turned up around you and your job." He leaned forward. "Not only did you raise some attention when you were involved with Garcia, there was a situation where you planted some information in a soldier's computer. That soldier later got court martialed, sent out because they couldn't connect that information with her actions. But there was enough info in those files for my partner and I to start looking at the Garcia death a little more closely."

Celie sat back then, letting him go on. "We've found enough information to reopen that case, Troy. To get you on trial for murder this time, not just manslaughter."

Evans' face paled even more, making him look gray. He started picking at a nail, his eyes going from Celie to Saint again, as if to find a chink in their argument.

"Who are you guys?"

"Didn't they tell you?" Saint drew out the moment.

When Evans shook his head, Saint introduced himself and turned his head to Celie. She stayed where she was, sitting in a faux relaxed position of her legs crossed and her hands in her lap. "And I'm Celie Garcia. Tony's sister."

Evans jerked back in his chair as if he had been hit. "You're shitting me."

"Nope. And I'm going to see that you stay in this prison for the rest of your life, Troy." She whispered and Saint wondered if they'd lost their chance.

"You can't prove anything," Evans whimpered.

"Maybe not," Saint inserted and leaned toward the glass, concealing his hand as he placed it on Celie's folded ones. "But we can make your life even more miserable than it is right now."

"How?" Evans moaned. "I'm in solitary confinement twenty three hours a day and when I'm not, I have a guard on my ass in the exercise yard. I've been stabbed two times and I'm not even sure why."

"Bullshit," Celie barked. "You've been stabbed because you were stupid and killed someone, bringing attention to yourself and your drug distribution." When Evans cast her a surprised glance, Celie continued. "You've been careless, Troy. You kill Tony, then get noticed by your superiors when you plant the files, and to cap it off, you kill another guy. What do you expect Fortner to do, let you skate by?"

Saint had to hand it to her, Celie could play a game as well as anybody.

"You guys ain't cops, MPs. You can't do anything to me."

"Oh, I know *we* can't. But we have a whole notebook full of stuff that connects you to Garcia's death. Enough that if we turn it over to the military, they'll have you in court so fast you'll not know what hit you. Oh, yeah, it'll be us." Celie smirked back at Evans and Saint bit back a curse. Damnit, Celie!

"You can't."

"I can and I will. Unless you tell me something."

"What?" Evans leaned closer. "I'll tell you how to make a bundle. You got connections? I can give you names, lots of them. Just deliver the goods to them and you'll be sitting on more money than your little ass can handle."

"We want names," Saint bit out, intent on getting Celie back on track. "We want the name of the man who's been after you. The man who was over your operation."

"You got it, man. Randy Fortner."

Celie started to comment but Saint talked over her in an effort to control the situation. "Where is he?"

"Hell if I know."

"Okay, how did you contact him before?" Saint pressed.

"I texted him. He gave me instructions, I followed them and then texted him." Evans looked at them and a gleam appeared in his eyes. "You want him? I can get to him. For a price."

"I think we'll just let you rot, Troy. Oh, but you won't be here that long, will you? Once Randy finds out we were here visiting, you'll be getting noticed, again."

Saint stood then and pulled Celie to his side, intent on getting out while they still could. Evans' curses and invectives followed them out of the room.

They were silent as they walked through the building from secured area to secured area and then past the last checkpoint. Finally, outside and in the parking lot, Saint took a cleansing breath of the hot, dry Kansas day and directed Celie toward the rental.

"Hell, Celie what did you think you were doing?" Saint opened the car door for Celie and stomped over to his.

Once in the rental, she cast him a tortured look. "I'm sorry. I let my emotions get carried away. If I hadn't goaded him, we might have gotten more info out of Troy."

"Yeah, there's that. But I'm more worried about the fact that you told him you had a notebook stuffed with information on his dealings, as well as Fortner's."

She paled under her tan. "I did? Oh, God, I did." She turned her gaze on the road before them. Saint figured she was reliving the conversation because she let out a curse of her own. "I didn't think. I'm sorry."

"Well, it's done. What we need to do now is get to a quiet place and get in touch with Hank."

They stopped at a small town between Leavenworth and Topeka. The motel was clean, had a microwave and fridge in the room and, best of all, was off the main road. Saint carried their stuff in and laid it on one of the double beds. Celie followed and plopped down on the other. "I feel like we're touring motels."

"Feels like it." He murmured and pulled out his phone. His shoulder was aching fiercely and he tried to keep the frustration out of his voice. Tank had left a message repeating his offer to help but Saint ignored it for now.

Hank Patterson picked up on the first ring. "How'd it go?"

"We got confirmation that Randy, or Randall, Fortner was Troy Evans' boss. I don't know if there is anyone above him, has to be, I guess. But I don't want to know unless we need to deal with them."

"Agreed." Hank said and continued. "I need to report this to the DEA, Saint. It's getting too big for us to handle on our own."

"I know. Keep me up on it and we can meet anyone we need to whenever."

"Where are you right now?"

Saint filled him in and then asked about the info he'd requested on Fortner. Again, he requested that no files be sent to him and he had Celie fill her notebook pages with yet more information that could get both of them killed.

At the end of the call, he tossed the phone onto the bed and eyed Celie. The long day's travel showed in the circles under her eyes and her rounded shoulders. Saint absorbed her discouragement and fear as if it were his own and determined, he had to make it right. At least for now.

"Let's go find something decent to eat." He slapped his knees and stood, reaching for his duffle.

"I'm not hungry." She said in a flat tone.

"I am and you get to come watch me eat." Saint held out his hand. "Come on. Take pity on me. The last meal I had was a boxed lunch."

She shrugged and let him pull her up then, taking her backpack, headed to the bathroom.

The restaurant they found was a barbecue place and Saint's mouth started watering before they got out of the car. The scent of smoke and meat wafted in the dry heat, advertising the food within. Celie's appetite reemerged with delivery of smoked meat and potatoes and they focused on the meal rather than small talk. Once finished, Saint found a convenience store and, with a look at Celie, went inside and purchased a couple packs of condoms.

They arrived at the motel as dusk was falling. Saint walked in after Celie and she saw him rubbing his left shoulder. It was the third time she'd noticed today. "Are you in pain?"

He shrugged. "The weather must be changing. My shoulder kinda hurts then. Don't worry about it."

"Will it help if you take it off for the evening?"

Saint glanced over at the laptop and then shook his head. Celie sighed. "You know, I can type as easily as you. You can write notes tonight and I'll do the searches."

He hesitated a moment then nodded and went into the bathroom. Celie wondered at that. They'd practically made out on the couch the night before and he'd had no qualms about her seeing his scars but he had to go into the bathroom to remove the artificial arm?

He returned, the arm in hand and his tshirt in place. Celie fiddled with her notebook, watching him plug the charging cord into the prosthesis surreptitiously. When he came to the built in desk carrying his laptop, she stepped up and took it from him. "You take the desk. I'm more comfortable on the bed."

She sat down and crossed her legs, settling the laptop on them and booted it up. With help from Saint for the password, she was in the primary search engine when he stopped her. "Let me have the computer for a minute."

She gave it to him with narrowed eyes and watched as he slowly typed in a string of letters and numbers. When he handed the device back to her she noticed a blank screen with a search bar only. "It's an encrypted site. And I'm using the phone as a hotspot, remember?"

She nodded, cursing herself at her naivete. "Okay. What do we search first?"

They searched for several hours, gleaning information on Randall Fortner, his past cities of residence, any publicity that featured his name, and more. By the time they finished for the night, Celie felt as if she knew the man Troy Evans was so afraid of. And for good reason.

"How has he escaped jail time?" Randall Fortner had no criminal record, as far as they could find. Nothing to link him officially to drug use, distribution or sales.

"He's smart." Saint said. "If you hadn't caught the link between him and Evans, we might not have figured it out. But, here's the thing, Celie." He leaned forward, his eyes serious. "If this guy is smart enough to evade the law for this long, he's smart enough to know someone is looking for him."

"But I haven't been looking for him. I was trying to find Troy Evans."

"Just as bad. He knows Evans was a sloppy operator and he's trying to get rid of him. With you looking for Evans, you've put yourself in the target zone."

She stared back at Saint, her heart thudding as she took in the ramifications of her actions. "So, I'm dead."

He jerked as if she'd slapped him. "Oh, hell no. We've just been given a great gift. We know who is out there gunning for you. Now all we have to do is find him first."

10

S aint reached out and closed the laptop then stood and held his hand out for it. When Celie handed it to him, he laid it on the desk and then turned his gaze on her. "You remember I stopped at the store after dinner?"

She nodded and gave him a small smile. "Your promised you would last night."

"They didn't have a value pack," he said as he pulled her up wrapped his arm around her. He kissed the smile on her lips and then deepened it, tasting her sweet mouth, taking in the honey taste so singular to Celie.

"They didn't?" She murmured into his mouth as her hands curled around his waist and cupped his ass.

"Nope. So I bought two packs," he rumbled and turning around, fell onto the bed with her landing on him with a laugh.

They spent time kissing. Saint couldn't remember the last time he'd taken his time getting to know a woman's mouth, the curve of her neck and jaw. He indulged in this pleasure with fierce intensity, sucking lightly at her skin and groaning when she did the same.

Once her nylon blouse was off, he spent time with her breasts, tasting and suckling. Her ribcage he found fascinating and he counted each small bump with his tongue, eliciting giggles from her. He found other places she was ticklish as well. The underside of her knee, the arches of her feet. And where she was sensitive. Her inner thighs and beyond. He took time to fit the condom before exploring more to both of their satisfaction.

Afterward, Saint lay on his stomach as she explored his back, her hands smoothing across his shoulders. He tensed as she neared the left one and then sighed at the feel of her lying full length on top of him. Her cheek lay in the indentation of his spine and her hair, that beautiful dark curly hair, spread over his right arm and hand as he lay with it bent on the mattress. "Are you still hurting?" She murmured and he chuckled.

"No. I think we found a cure, baby." At her answering laugh, he continued. "I like this position and all but it kind of restricts me, you know."

Her hand smoothed over his shoulder and he felt her, even through the numbed scars. His body became goose flesh in response. "But I like this mattress."

"I'm sure you do," he reached behind him and captured her thigh, then rolled over until she was flush against him, chest to chest, groin to groin. "That's better," he wrapped his arm around her and closed his eyes.

"That's what you rolled me over like a carp for? To sleep?" She huffed in mock annoyance.

"Just give me a couple minutes, baby."

The couple minutes lasted for forty five. Celie lay on Saint and watched him sleep, dream. She lay content for several minutes then peeled herself off him and went to the bathroom. Upon returning to the bed, she noted he'd spread out over the entire sleeping area, like a starfish, his arm and legs spread out. She crept around the room til she located her underwear and a tshirt before retreating to the other bed where she fell into a deep sleep, unbothered by dreams.

Halfway through the night, he joined her and made love to her, slowly and thoroughly. When he turned on his side toward her and pulled her to him, Celie decided to leave well enough alone. Obviously, they would sleep together tonight.

The morning dawned with the smell of coffee. Celie opened her eyes to find a Styrofoam cup on the nightstand and she reached out for it before sitting up.

"You don't function without it either, do you?" Saint sat at the desk, fully dressed and with his prosthesis in place. A tray of what looked like pancakes sat in front of him and he was eating with obvious enjoyment.

She grunted and frowned at his grin. When he gestured toward the other bed, she saw another covered tray sitting on it. "I got you a big breakfast. I didn't know if you like sweet or savory for breakfast."

"I like both," she said.

After a bathroom visit, Celie ate the fast food breakfast, grateful for Saint's thoughtfulness. As her head cleared and the impact of the previous day returned, she laid down her fork. "Do we have to worry about Fortner today?"

"I think we need to worry about Fortner and, even though he's in prison, Evans. We have our packs and are armed, even if we haven't practiced in a few days. Hopefully they won't be able to locate us here, though. I don't think Fortner's web extends to rental car agencies."

"But you found a lot of information on the computer. Don't you think he might be able to as well?" She pressed.

"Maybe. But I doubt Evans was able to get his information out as quickly as he'd like. We may have today to rest and recoup before we have to set out again."

Celie stood and took the rest of her tray to the trash can and dumped it then washed her hands. "And where do we go from here?"

"We're going to California. The last place you were posted."

Hank called that morning as they sat and reviewed Celie's notes. The DEA wanted to meet with them at the Landon State Office Building later that day. As they packed up once again Celie idly thought, she'd been more stable on a military base in the middle of the desert. At least she'd had the same bed for several nights there.

Topeka was blaring and busy, compared to the towns they'd spent their time in over the past few days. By the time Celie and Saint got into to see Agent Simpson, she had a headache and wished for a long cleansing run.

Brian Simpson wasted no time in niceties but got straight to the point. "I've heard you have some information on Randall Fortner."

Saint and Celie exchanged glances and then turned to Simpson. "Probably not what you want," Saint said and they discussed the information he and Celie had been able to dredge up. When they mentioned the connection Celie had made earlier that week, Simpson's brows raised and he went from listening as a courtesy to attending to them with sharp intensity.

"Do you have any substantial proof?" He demanded, his hand gripping an ink pen.

Celie shook her head. "I don't think so."

He leaned back and tilted his head to study her. "What was the information that was planted in your computer?"

She shook her head again, "I don't know. I was only told it detailed something that led to a suspicion of drug dealing."

The agent frowned, "And they used that to discharge you?"

She shrugged. "It must have been sufficient. I didn't have any marks against my job, nothing personal either."

"Do you think there might have been something in the paperwork on Celie's computer?" Saint said with a frown.

"Possibly. Otherwise, why would someone come after her?" When Saint mentioned Evans, Simpson waved his hand in dismissal. "Evans isn't important. He's expendable. What would make Fortner and his people take notice of someone would be information that would implicate them." He turned back to Celie. "You need to request a record of your hearing."

She cursed to herself. "I did. It was destroyed in a fire several days ago. But it didn't have anything pertaining to the documents, other than mention of them."

"They would have had to have been introduced as evidence," Simpson said and Saint nodded then pulled out his phone.

"Who are you calling?"

"My boss," Saint said and put the phone to his ear.

"We can subpoena the documents."

"It's faster this way," Saint assured him.

He asked Hank for the documents and was assured they'd be in Simpson's mailbox by the afternoon. In the meantime, Hank and Celie spent several minutes assuring Simpson they had had nothing happen to them since leaving Mississippi and didn't need extra protection.

Hank's sources came through in record time and Simpson opened the file, followed by a groan. "It's in military language."

Celie and Saint shared a grin and she offered to glance over the information for the agent. With some reluctance, Simpson vacated his chair to her and Celie quickly read over the information. "It looks like a distribution schedule. Loads of supplies going to different overseas posts." She turned her head to take in both Saint and Simpson, her expression tight. "It was facilitated by a soldier that we had on our list. His supervisor was Evans."

"And Fortner?" Agent Simpson pressed.

Celie shook her head. "No. His name isn't on there, and if you didn't look into the temporary postings, you wouldn't connect Evan's man to him either."

"So, there's a listing of all the sites for distribution?" Saint asked, his forehead creasing.

"Yes." Celie found the listings and pointed to them. "Here is one that I was posted at in the Middle East. I remember the court questioning me on the dates I was there. I guess they connected me and the documents through that posting." She marveled at the efficiency of the list. "If they were, or are, distributing drugs to all these bases? They're making a killing."

"And would be willing to do whatever they have to do to insure that no one interferes with that job." Saint growled.

11

Saint kept his hand on Celie's back as they exited the office building. His blood, which always seemed to run hotter when around Celie, now froze in his veins. She'd unleashed a swarm with her investigation and now, he had to keep her safe until he got her to Hank.

She turned to look at him and frowned, "What is it?"

"Change of plans," he said as he opened the car door for her.

"What? We're going to California, right?"

He shook his head as he backed out of the parking space and into traffic. "We're going to Montana."

"Montana. What's there?"

"Hank Patterson and a whole lot of bad asses that might keep you alive until Simpson and his crew find Fortner." He looked for the sign toward Kansas City.

"You're taking me to Montana for some guys to protect me?" Her voice ended an octave higher and significantly louder than before. "You're crazy."

"No, I'm trying to keep you alive." He changed lanes and kept driving, ignoring the outraged look on her face.

"What happened to 'we're prepared' and 'we've got enough protection with us'?"

"That was before I saw the size of this operation. This isn't just a couple of guys who are selling drugs to soldiers, Celie. This is a massive operation, complete with its own army."

She sat back in her seat and stared at the traffic around them. Finally, she said quietly. "Take me to the airport and I'll take care of everything else."

He shook his head, laughing bitterly. "With what? We're on Hank's dime, remember? You don't have enough money to go anywhere else."

She didn't answer him and they drove past a sign indicating that Kansas City lay fifty odd miles away. Saint shifted and removed his phone from his back pocket, called Hank to arrange another private plane trip, then lay it on the console between them. As he drove, he was aware of her beside him, of her resignation and her simmering anger, mixed with fear. Fear he understood, but the anger? Why would she be angry at him for trying to protect her?

She leaned back and propped her knees up against the glove compartment and picked up his phone. She swiped the screen and typed in some prompts which brought up a short video. Saint sighed with relief. Finally, she'd realized he was right.

CELIE WENT through several silly videos before she was sure Saint wouldn't be monitoring her actions on the phone, then brought up the airport website. As soon as she found the information she needed, she backed out and played around with the phone for several minutes more then disconnected. The signal, spotty as Saint drove, had lasted as long as she needed, thank God. Now, she needed to see if she had enough money.

They reached the airport by late afternoon. Saint turned in the car to the rental agency and reached for Celie's back-pack only to find she had it shouldered already. "Ready to go?" She prompted and they walked toward the main building.

Celie took note of the buses and taxis as they walked and mentally calculated once again. If she could get in touch with her Dad, she'd be okay. If she could get into the city, that is.

Saint located the section which housed the gates for private flights and they went to a large concourse to sit and wait. Celie sat for a few minutes then glancing at Saint, said, "I could go for a cup of coffee. What about you?"

He started to rise then sat back when she stood. "I'll get it." She shrugged, "I don't have any money."

He smiled and handed her a twenty. She'd kept her backpack on and started down the gate and then turned when he called to her. "I'll keep your backpack for you."

She laughed and waved it off. "I'm used to it by now. I'll be back in a couple minutes."

The twenty would get her into town, she figured, then she find the bus station, a place her dad could wire her some money, and she'd be set.

SAINT LOOKED AT HIS WATCH. Ten minutes had passed and still no Celie. The rock in his gut that had formed as he watched her walk away started rolling around, making friends. He shouldered his laptop bag and picked up his duffle and walked the wide causeway, looking right and left. As he did, he dialed Hank.

"Yeah?"

"I've lost her."

Silence met him for a solid minute before Hank responded in a quiet voice. "Lost her?"

"Yeah." Saint stopped in the middle of the causeway, people parting around him like a river yielding to a stone. "She said she was going to get coffee and disappeared."

"Where are you?"

"At the Kansas City airport, waiting for the plane." Saint started walking again and filled Hank in as he scanned for Celie's lean figure.

"So, she was okay with coming out here?"

"She said she was." But, obviously, she hadn't been. Saint cursed and looked around, finally finding a kiosk where he asked the woman behind the register where the taxis and buses were stationed. Then he started sprinting. "She had twenty bucks. She can't go far on that."

"She got any family or friends to ask to wire money?" Hank's reply brought forth a string of curses and Saint broke into a dead run.

A bus rounded the end of the lane as he came to a heaving stop and he glanced around, looking for a taxi. When he found one, the driver asked for a destination. Saint hesitated then said, "Drive toward the city. I'll let you know." He called Celie's burn phone. When he didn't get an answer, he leaned forward. "Where's the closest Western Union?"

"There's a few in the city. Which one you want?"

"Hell, the closest one to the bus station, I guess." Saint drew his hand over his head in exasperation.

"That's easy. There's one in the bus station itself. I'll get you there in a few minutes."

The few minutes crawled as Saint stared out into the

early evening. He took in every pedestrian, every cop on the street, resented every stop light they encountered. When the guy pulled into the front of the building Saint thanked him curtly and exited. "Good travels," the driver called and pulled away from the curb.

When he got to the Western Union kiosk, Saint drew in a breath of relief. Celie was seated nearby, her head down and her eyes on her backpack, resting in her lap. As if she felt his eyes on her, she looked up and Saint felt the stone in his insides chip away.

She looked more lonely and desolate than he'd ever seen her. As he approached, her eyes filled with tears. "My dad is in the hospital."

Saint dropped onto the chair beside her and took her in his arms, backpack and all. She laid her head on his shoulder and he idly wished he'd sat on her left side so she didn't have metal to rest against. "What happened?"

"An accident they said. When I called his house, a neighbor answered. She was watching Dad's dog, Sarge. She said he'd been there for a couple of days. They'd been trying to reach me." She drew in a shuddering breath. "I called him after the fire but didn't tell him anything about it. I guess he hadn't kept my new number." With that, her control broke and she sobbed into his shirt.

Saint let her go until he could feel her breaths calm into some semblance of rhythm and then a few minutes more, until she took a breath that didn't contain a break. "Where is he?"

"Tampa."

"Okay. Let's go." He gently pushed her away and stood, then offered her his hand.

"To Tampa?"

"To Tampa."

This time she got on the plane. Saint made sure Celie had something to drink since she spent most of the flight wiping at her eyes. He spent the time wondering if the accident she didn't seem to know anything about was really an accident or if her father had fallen into the same trap she had. And if he had, how would Celie react, knowing her actions could have put her father at risk?

IT TOOK them a few minutes to find her father's room. When they did, Celie hesitated at the door, then entered, Saint trailing behind her. Anthony Garcia lay in the bed, swathed in bandages. He bore one on his right arm and a splint covered his wrist and hand. Another bandage wrapped around his head. His hospital gown drooped on one shoulder and yet another bandage could be seen underneath that. Celie tried to breathe, tried to stop the gray that threatened to take over her sight.

Saint's hand on her back brought her back to alertness and she approached her father's bed. "Dad?"

Her father's eyes, rimmed with dark circles, were closed but as she bent close to him, fluttered as if he were trying to wake.

"Dad. It's Celie. Can you hear me?" She ended the question in a whisper of panic. What if he never woke? "Papi?"

Saint turned around and exited the room, leaving her stroking her father's whiskered cheek. It was cool from the air in the room, or from not moving. She rounded the bed, surveying his bandages and wondering what had happened.

Saint returned with a nurse following behind him, her expression one of exasperation, as if he'd pulled her from another patient's bed. "He said you have some questions," she gestured toward Saint with a jerk of her head.

"Yes. Is my father unconscious? I tried to wake him but I couldn't."

The nurse glanced at Saint again and then tempered her tone. "He's not my patient but let me go check."

Celie, at her father's side, put her hand atop his as it rested flat on the bed. An oxygen monitor was clamped on his finger and an IV attached to his forearm, leaving her precious little room to hold his hand. She curved her fingers around his hand and squeezed. "I'm here, Papi. I'm here now."

When the nurse returned, she had another one, a male nurse, in tow. After introducing them, she fled, leaving the three of them in the room. "Can I help?"

"I'm his daughter. Could you tell me what has happened and how he's doing?"

The nurse came forward and, as if he couldn't help himself, started checking monitors, IV drips and bandages. "He apparently was mugged. Came in a couple days ago. I think a neighbor found him in his yard. He has a concussion and a broken arm. We thought he might have broken ribs too but they were just bruised."

Celie's other hand covered her midsection. "And is he unconscious?"

"No. We gave him something for his pain. He's not been getting much sleep in the past couple days, what with us having to wake him every couple hours to do a cognition check. He finally got through that, as well as the respiratory dangers, so I gave him something to help him rest." The nurse checked his watch and smiled at her. "He'll be coming out of it in an hour or so, if you want to come back."

She settled against the wall, her hand still covering her father's. "I'll wait."

"Okay. I'll see if I can round up another chair for you

and your friend." He left and Celie looked at Saint. "Dad would never get mugged."

"Celie, it happens in all cities."

She shook her head vehemently. "Not to my father. He's kept up his PE ever since he left the Army. He runs every day, lifts weights, hikes. Saint, he's in better shape than most thirty year olds."

"If someone comes up on you—"

"It would have had to be more than one person. It had to have been." She trailed off and watched her father breathe. Saint didn't understand. Her father was one of the biggest, bravest and most together men she'd ever known. He wouldn't have let someone best him in a one on one. Not her dad.

After an aide brought in a straight backed plastic chair, Saint made her sit, even though she wouldn't leave her father's side. She sank into the chair and leaned her head against the raised head of the bed and prayed. Prayed as if she'd never prayed before. Prayed that she hadn't caused her father's injuries.

12

Anthony came out of his deep sleep as suddenly as if a light switch had been flicked on. Saint stood at the end of the bed, staring out at the cars entering and leaving the entrance when a husky voice grated, "Who are you?"

He turned and gestured toward Celie, who was asleep, her head resting against her father's bed. "Her friend."

Anthony's head dropped to one side and he caught sight of his daughter. "She looks pretty worn out."

"She's been worried about you," Saint replied in a low tone. If Celie could continue to sleep through this, he'd be grateful. "The nurse said you were mugged."

"Mugged, hell. Someone targeted me. Three guys jumped me in my own damned yard." Saint almost smiled at the man's look of disgust. Celie hadn't been far off the mark. This man was still Army in a lot of ways.

"You know them?"

Anthony shook his head then winced. "No. I didn't see one of them, he was behind me all the time. But I got a good look at the other two."

"Have you talked to the police?"

"I did yesterday. They said they'd bring in some pictures for me to look at. I think they were afraid I'd die or something if they waited til I got out of the hospital." He glanced at Celie again. "My neighbor said they couldn't get in touch with Celie. What happened?"

"Her rental was destroyed in a fire." Saint didn't elaborate but then, apparently, he didn't have to.

Anthony narrowed his eyes. "Was it set?" At Saint's nod, he cursed. "She started looking into Tony's death. Is this what all this is from?"

Saint nodded again. "And she's going to hate herself when she finds out you were injured as part of that."

Anthony gingerly moved his head into another shake. "Doesn't matter. I've been hurt before, I healed then and I'll heal now. And I'm on notice. The thing that matters now is to find the bastard who killed my son." He paused and then added, "And ruined her future."

Celie stirred and lifted her head, bringing her hand to her mouth as if to check to see if she'd been drooling. Saint smiled and motioned toward her father. She stood and bent to kiss Anthony on the cheek.

"I think I'll go see if I can find some coffee. You two want anything?" When they both shook their heads, Saint headed out of the room, intent to give them some time. He returned with a newspaper, a soft drink and an outdoor magazine. When he entered, Celie was sitting on the edge of the bed laughing with her father. Another, older woman stood on the other side of the bed. Her smile faded a bit at the sight of Saint's prosthesis but returned to its wide friendliness a second later.

"Saint, this is Maggie. She's Dad's neighbor and the one I talked to earlier."

Saint nodded to the woman who murmured a greeting. Anthony Garcia stuck out his uninjured hand. "Celie tells me you've been helping her out over the past week or so."

Had it only been that long? Saint counted the days, less than a week. He knew Celie better than women he'd dated for months and felt she knew him as well. "Sir."

"You got another name?"

"Luc Benatou."

"Get your name in the services?"

Saint nodded, "Army."

Anthony indicated his prosthesis. "Looks like you came home with a souvenir too."

"Dad!" Celie's shock came through loud and clear.

"Well, hell, honey. He's got to have heard worse."

Saint chuckled. He had indeed. "It works pretty good. Popular at Halloween when I dress up like an android."

Anthony laughed then groaned. "Maggie, you mind taking Celie down to the cafeteria and getting some coffee?"

Celie lifted her brow. "I'm not going anywhere, Dad. You want to talk to Saint, you'll do it with me in the room."

Maggie glanced from one to the other and then to the third person and shrugged and shouldered a tapestry bag. "I'm going to go, Tony. I'll check in with you tomorrow, okay?" She leaned down and kissed his cheek then rose, a blush on her own cheeks.

"Okay. Don't let Sarge get away with too much."

"Oh, you know me. I'm a tough mother." She chuckled and left.

"She'll have fed him steak and eggs for breakfast every morning by the time I leave this place." Anthony grumbled then turned his gaze on Celie. "You gonna tell me what you've been up to?"

She stood ramrod straight and met his gaze straight and proud. "I've been looking into Tony's death."

"And you found something." Anthony nodded.

"We've found that he unearthed some details about drug shipments to the Middle East. And got killed for it." She stated baldly. Her father stared down at his bandaged arm. "Go on."

"Tony's killer was the one who planted the files in my account at work. I found that out by bribing some Army guys I used to work with. Then, when Saint joined me, we found out who that guy's boss was in the drug organization."

"And found out you've unearthed a den of snakes." Anthony pressed.

"Not unearthed them yet." Saint said. "They're still underground but we're pretty sure we've stirred them up enough to start looking at Celie as a threat."

"And your house? Saint said it was destroyed." Her father shifted a little in the bed and Celie moved to adjust his pillow. At his request, she lowered the head slightly.

"It was deliberately set afire or bombed. We heard a blast but that might have been something that blew up after the fire caught. Either way, everything was destroyed."

"Where were you?" He asked, his tone sharp.

"We went running," she assured him. "That's why no one could reach me. My phone was in the trailer, along with my purse, everything. Saint here has been covering costs for the whole search."

Saint waved off Anthony's offer to compensate him. Whomever had hired him would cover the expenses, or he'd do so.

"So, that the only time somebody tried to hurt you? Or warn you off?"

Celie hesitated a moment too long before replying.

"Someone shot at us in Mississippi after the fire. Since then, no."

"But they found you," Saint rounded the bed and stood at Anthony's side.

"Yep. They found me. And I think this," Anthony gestured at his arm, then his head, "was an effort to get Celie here. And it damned well worked."

Celie looked up, startled only to find both men's gazes locked on her. "Me? Oh, Dad."

Anthony's lips thinned and he stared into space. "If they wanted to get you here, the easiest way was to get to me. It worked obviously. Now, we have to figure out what their next move is going to be."

"They might expect her to go to your place," Saint said quietly and Anthony threw him a sharp look.

"Call Maggie. Tell her to take Sarge to her house. She was going to stay at mine tonight because he does better at home."

He rattled off a number and Saint started dialing. He looked up as he finished. "Did she stay there every night since you've been in the hospital?"

"Yeah."

"They've probably been watching the house to see who is coming and going, so she's probably okay. But I'd feel better if she was at her own home as well."

Saint moved away to speak to Maggie and Celie covered her father's bandaged arm with her hand. "Dad, I'm sorry I did this to you."

"You don't apologize. I should have started the search for the bastard who killed Tony myself, instead of letting you do it. I guess I've been too deep in my own head."

She shook her head, "It's gotten too out of hand. I shouldn't have started it in the first place."

"Hindsight, mija, hindsight. What we need to worry about right now is how the hell we're going to get out of this situation with our skins intact."

"And the bastards behind bars." She added.

"That too, if we're lucky."

Saint stood at the end of the room, watching Celie and her father as they caught up. The affection between the two was obvious, as well as the respect each had for the other. He fiddled with his phone for a few minutes then turned away from the bed and dialed Hank's number.

"Hey, what's up?"

"Celie's father was attacked a few days ago."

"Damn it," Hank bit out. "Is he all right?"

"Pretty beat up, has a concussion and a broke arm. Listen, we think the attack might have been a tool to bring Celie to Florida."

"And you're there now." Hank said. "You need some back up?"

"Yeah, that's why I was calling. I guess we need to contact the local cops or DEA too, just in case."

"We can worry about them after we get our men in place. When is Celie's dad being released?"

"Not sure. The doctor hasn't been in to check on him lately."

"Call me back with that info. You okay to cover him and Celie while he's in the hospital?"

Saint glanced around the room. It was small and could be easily defended, unless someone came in with guns blazing, which he didn't expect. "I think we're good."

"I'll get to work on my end. Fill me in when you get some news."

Saint assured him he would then, before Hank hung up,

he asked the question that had been on his mind over the past couple hours. "Hank, who's footing the bill for this?"

"Huh?"

"Who's the client? I know it's not Celie. Don't think it's her father, either. So, who's paying for this?"

"I can't tell you that right now," Hank said, his voice even.

"Will you be able to fill me in later?"

"Possibly."

Saint disconnected then and turned to find both Celie and her father watching him with alert expressions. "Hank's going to send someone down to help out."

Celie nodded. "Good." She stood and stretched, "You hungry Dad? Do you want me to run down to the cafeteria and get you something?"

"No." Both Saint and Anthony responded. When Celie turned to glance at Saint, he shrugged. "We need to both stay here. Maybe Anthony's friend will bring us something to eat and a toothbrush."

Celie studied him and then nodded. "Okay. We hole up here for a while. Just another stop on our motel tour."

She and Saint laughed but Anthony stared at them with narrowed eyes. "How long you two been traveling together?"

"Dad!" Celie protested, eliciting another chuckle from Saint.

13

They spent the night in the room, each trying to catch naps in their chairs. Saint, for one, would rather have laid on the desert floor than sit in the straight backed chair and nap. He ended up stretching out on the floor at the end of the room and sleeping a couple hours while Celie sat watch.

Anthony cat napped as well, waking each time a nurse or aide entered the room. All three checked and rechecked the personnel and watched as Anthony's IV was removed, turned backs so his catheter was removed in relative privacy, and monitored him as he received and took antibiotics. If the nurses thought Celie and Saint were overprotective of her father, they didn't say, only going about their jobs as efficiently as ever.

The morning brought Saint almost pleading for some coffee from the nurses. He'd downed the first cup without tasting it, aiming for the caffeine to jumpstart his brain cells. The second cup, thoughtfully brought to them by an older volunteer, resulted in his being able to plan. When the doctor came by to discharge Anthony, all three adults in the room were more than ready.

Since most of his clothing had been removed with scissors, Anthony had to call Maggie and ask if she could bring him some clothes. First, however, he called another friend. Celie tried to listen to him as he walked gingerly to the bathroom but a snarl and the door shutting in her face sent her to the small closet and the task of gathering his few personal items.

An hour later, Maggie strode in with a small satchel, followed by a brute of a man. He carried another bag, similar in size but with a small lock on it. When Celie saw the man she uttered a cry of pleasure. "Uncle Bud!"

She ran over to the man and hugged him, getting a squeeze in return. When he pulled back, he frowned down at her. "Why'd you not call me when you started all this, C?"

"Started all what, Bud?" She took the small satchel from Maggie and, knocking on the bathroom door, handed it through to her father after he opened for her.

"This fool mission you set out on. You know you could have called me and your dad in on this. We'd have helped you handle it. Not get blind sided by it."

She sighed and apologized. "Sorry, Uncle Bud. I didn't think. Let me introduce you to Saint. Luc Benatou, this is my dad's friend, Bud Lincoln. They served in the Army together."

"Sir," Saint held out his hand to shake and Bud engulfed it with his huge paw of a hand.

"No sir about it. I never made it past Sargent. Not like Anthony. He made Sargent Major."

Saint lifted his eyebrow. One of the top NCO ranks, Sargent Major status meant a leader on the field. Most of the other Sargent Majors he'd met were bad asses both on the field and at home. Celie smiled at him, knowing her pride in her father showed through.

"We talking about ancient history?" Anthony came out of the bathroom, fully dressed in jeans and an opened button up shirt. "Somebody wanta help me with this? I can't do up the damn things with one hand."

Celie stepped forward, only to be waylaid by Maggie who deftly buttoned Anthony's shirt. Surprised and a little jealous, Celie smiled at Maggie's blush when she turned away. Anthony cleared his throat and pointed to the satchel. "I guess I'll need help with the shoes too."

As Maggie busied herself helping Anthony tie his shoes, he glanced over her head and leveled a gaze at Bud. "You bring it?"

Bud held up the bag. "Just like you said."

Anthony looked over at Saint and Celie. "You got your weapons?"

Maggie started and glanced up at the crew in the room. "Weapons?"

"It's okay, honey. We're just being careful." Anthony patted her shoulder and she eyed him then stood from her crouch and put her hands on her hips.

"You know better than to patronize me, Anthony Garcia. If you think there's going to be trouble, you need to say so. I may not carry a gun or shoot, but at least I need to be alert enough to hide when I need to."

Celie bit back a smile at her father's expression. He looked like Maggie had just told him she was going to join the circus. "She's right, Dad. If she's going to be near any of us, she needs to be kept informed, too. And yes, Saint and I have our guns and we have carry permits, or at least I do. But not in Florida."

"Mine is from Louisiana," Saint said.

"Well, hell. We're all law abiding citizens," Bud groused and handed the satchel over to Anthony then fished around in his jeans' pocket and extracted a small ring of keys. He handed those over as well.

Saint's phone trilled as Anthony laid the satchel on the bed and began shuffling through the keys. Celie monitored each as Saint completed a short but apparently satisfying call. Midway through he asked for Anthony's address and relayed it to the caller and then hung up with a gratified expression. "We're going to be all set in about thirty minutes."

Anthony glanced up from fumbling with the keys and held them out to Celie. "You want to do this, Celie? I'm all thumbs."

As she unlocked the satchel and removed the pistol, she cast him a worried look. "You think you can handle this, Dad? With your arm and all?"

He looked disgusted and held out his hand for the gun. "The day I can't handle a pistol is the day I go into a home."

She shook her head at him. "Right." She was just closing the satchel with the extra rounds and yet another pistol when a nurse entered with a transport technician and a wheelchair. Several minutes of argument later, a cane was produced and Anthony Garcia exited the hospital under his own steam as well as a contingent of his own bodyguards.

At the parking lot, Saint, along with Bud, crawled under the cars and looked for anything that was unusual. As no one in the party were bomb experts, Celie wondered if that was a bit of overkill, but she demurred and let the men do what they would. Her worry, more than a bomb in the car chassis, was the open lot and the abundance of places a shooter could conceal himself.

Celie insisted her father ride in the car with Bud on the

way to his house. They'd decided, though Fortner's people may have the house under surveillance, it was the most familiar piece of ground they could defend. And, Saint added, as he put the car into gear, Hank's men would meet them there.

Celie drew in a breath as she saw the street come into view. The bright Florida sunshine bounced heat back off the pavement and sparse grass struggled to grow in the sandy soil of yards. Two black SUVs were parked to either side of the house. "Not trying to be subtle, are they?" She said as they neared the driveway to the small one story house. Saint pulled through the driveway and into the rear yard, followed by Bud.

"No need. Hank wants Fortner and his bunch to know the house is covered."

"Let's hope they get the message." Celie said and, making sure her gun was secured in her back waistband, exited the car to meet her father.

They made it into the house in record time, even though Anthony still walked gingerly, pushing his bruised body as hard as he could. Saint and Bud scoured the inside before they let anyone in and Celie stood with her back to her father, taking in the quiet yard and houses next door. When a neighbor on the opposite site of Maggie's house stuck his head out of the door and yelled a hello to Anthony, Celie started and grimaced at her father's look of displeasure. "Take it easy, Celie. Don't shoot my poker partner."

"Sorry." She muttered an raised her hand in mute hello when Charlie, the neighbor greeted her. Anthony refused his offer to come over and keep him company. "Celie and her man's here for a couple of days. Maybe after that."

"Sure thing. Just give me a call. Need some time away from Jennie, you know."

When Saint tapped Anthony on the shoulder and he ushered Maggie inside, followed by Celie, she gave a sigh of relief. She could handle this, she had to.

In the living room, Anthony lowered his body slowly into his recliner and leaned his head against the leather back. Maggie, hovering, offered coffee, tea and beer before he irritably told her he was fine and she needed to either sit down or go home. She shook her head at Celie and took a seat on the sofa then, with a hand to her chest, said, "Sarge. I need to go home and get Sarge."

"Give me a few minutes, Maggie. When he gets here, he'll be all over me." Anthony sighed and closed his eyes. Celie watched him and noted the white tinge around his lips. "Dad, you need to lie down?"

"No. I want to be here. Just give me a few minutes. Maggie, could you get me a couple of aspirin?" He leaned forward and removed the gun from his waistband then placed it on the small table beside his chair.

Resigned that sitting and resting was the best she could hope for, Celie went in search of Saint and Bud. Bud, she found in the bedroom, his bulk shadowed by the window curtains and his gaze taking in the street before him. "Never thought I'd be playing Kandahar chicken here."

Celie tried a smile but the vision his words brought to mind, of fighting in the streets and innocent lives being sacrificed made her blood run cold. She turned and kept looking for Saint. The guest bedroom, the one reserved for her visits, was empty and neat, as always. Another window, this one facing the rear of the property, would serve as another vantage point, if need be.

Saint was in the kitchen with his phone to his ear. He turned at her entrance and held his hand out to her. Celie automatically advanced and clasped the artificial hand and, to her embarrassment, gave it a squeeze. Saint continued his conversation, then hung up. He looked at her then and what he found must have bothered him.

"You okay?"

She nodded and released him. "Bud just reminded me of something I'd rather not think about right now. Who was that? Hank's guys?"

"No, I talked to them just a few minutes ago. They're looking around the block then they'll take turns coming in and introducing themselves." At her nod he continued. "I was talking to Hank just now."

"And?"

"And Fortner was seen in Chicago a couple days ago."

"A couple of days are plenty of time to travel here, Saint."

"I know. And so does Hank. He did give me another piece of news."

His expression was set, his eyes intent on her. "Yes?" She asked impatiently, wanting to get back to the living room where she could keep an eye on her father and the street as well.

"Troy Evans was killed yesterday."

14

S aint eyed Celie as she sat in a chair she'd dragged in from the kitchen. She'd positioned it to the side of the living room window and surveyed the street in front of Anthony's house. It had been several hours since he'd told her of Troy Evans' death. Though he was in solitary, for some reason, Troy had been allowed to use a shower room that evening and had been found with his throat slashed, bleeding out into the shower drain.

Saint had watched the blood leech from Celie's cheeks and her eyes turn dark and fearful. She knew, as he did, that if Evans had been approached, he would have spilled everything he knew about them, about Celie's information. About her search for vengeance. Now, as dusk began to fall, Saint had the feeling they were going to find out how serious Randy Fortner was in ridding himself of the irritant Celie had become.

He glanced at his phone and the text that appeared. No new movement, per Hank's north and south guys. No movement on the street, other than the usual traffic, according to Maggie. Anthony, as much as he wanted to help, had spent the afternoon napping in his recliner and now looked as if he needed an unbroken night's sleep.

Saint noted Maggie, seated on the sofa, was looking weary. "Maggie, you want me to take you home?"

She shook her head and, glancing toward Anthony, smiled. "I'd just worry. I'm fine here. Except, I do need someone to either go feed Sarge or to bring him back home. I don't want to think of what he'll do if he's left in that house without food tonight."

Saint smiled. "What kind of dog is he?" He imagined a German Shepherd or Lab but Maggie laughed and pulled out her phone. She scrolled through some pictures before pulling up Sarge. Saint grinned at the photo of Maggie and Anthony, seated on the ground with a dog between them. The closed eyes and wide smile on the bulldog's face told Saint how spoiled the animal was in one shot. "Not much of a watchdog, huh?"

"Oh, you'd be surprised. If Sarge had been in the front yard with Anthony, I don't think we'd have had the result we do now."

"Why don't I go over and get him," Saint said.

Maggie shook her head. "If you go in the house, he'll see you as an intruder. He hasn't been introduced to you, so he wouldn't see you as a friend. It'll have to be me."

"Let me go, Maggie. I can bring him home and if you need anything, I'd be happy to bring it as well." Celie stood and Saint saw the restless energy burning in her. After a lukewarm protest, Maggie gave in and handed Celie her keys. "I don't think I need anything, thanks. I have things over here that I can use."

Celie leveled a look at Maggie that held questions but kept silent and strode toward the kitchen. "I'll go the back way. Won't be a minute."

. . .

MAGGIE'S HOUSE was built on the same snug floorplan as her father's and, as she passed through a gate that had been added in the dividing fence, Celie wondered how long her father and Maggie had been seeing each other. Both had lived in the neighborhood for years, but Celie had never imagined more than friendship would come for the pair. A widower, Anthony hadn't indicated his need or desire to find another partner, as far as Celie knew. But there you had it. Life came with surprises.

She unlocked the door, marveling at the ease of the mechanism. In the sultry summer heat, her father's door often stuck and had to be shouldered open. Once inside, she flicked on the kitchen light and surveyed the room.

The dog dish, empty and pushed into the middle of the room indicated Sarge's frustration with being left in a house alone with no food. She smiled then wondered at the silence. Sarge always bounded to the source of movement in any situation, whether it was a squirrel outside the window or a firefight on television. Yet, now, the house was as silent as a tomb.

Just as she started to pull her pistol from her back, Celie heard a sound. A whimper? She strode toward the living room where she saw the dog lying on its side, blood pooling beneath it.

"Sarge!" Celie ran to the dog and knelt beside him, her hand automatically covering the small hole she saw in his side. The blood underneath him was dark, as if it had set for a while and the dog wasn't moving.

"Poor thing. I didn't want to shoot him, but dogs can be a problem, you know."

Celie felt her pistol being pulled from her waistband as

she turned her head to take in the man standing behind her. Another, larger, man was standing by the front door, his pistol leveled at Celie.

"Cecilia Garcia. I'd like to say it's a pleasure, but then I'd be lying, wouldn't I?"

"Fortner?" She hoped her voice didn't sound as scared as she was at this moment. How had he managed to come here, unnoticed by them all? He was nondescript. Medium build, medium height, medium brown hair and eyes. Someone who could easily blend in with his surroundings. Is that how he managed to evade everyone?

"No. Unfortunately, Mr. Fortner has had some difficulty in management. He's been reprimanded."

Celie felt a slight rising of Sarge's side under her hand. She smoothed her fingers over the part of his coat that wasn't wet with blood and tried to think, even as she knew she needed to keep this man talking. He appeared cocky enough not to be in a hurry.

"You're his boss?" She wanted to bite her tongue even as the words came.

"Now, I wouldn't want to divulge any information, Cecilia. Not that it matters, I guess. Yes. I am. And I think you figured out that Fortner was Evans' superior, as well."

"You had Troy killed." She looked over his shoulder at the guard standing by the door. He hadn't moved, had twitched a muscle. Hadn't lowered his gun, either.

"I believe in efficiency, Cecilia. Troy Evans showed time and time again that he wasn't paying attention to the details. When he fucked up the shipments and then brought attention to the supply department with his rash actions with the loader? I let that go, since I was assured he'd take care of the situation. But when he planted the information in your computer, I figured it was time for him to go."

"You knew about that?" She said, her surprise making her forget to be cautious.

"Not until after the fact. Troy was negligent. He didn't check your credentials out before he planted the files. If he'd been smart, he'd have found someone with a smudge or two on their record or, better yet, one of his distributors. But he was in a hurry and for some reason, felt resentful toward your brother and, since you were his sister, you."

"Because he knew Tony would have turned the information over to his superior."

"Probably. And that would have been Troy's worst nightmare. And not great for me, either."

She looked down at the dog, worried that the shallow breaths she saw were getting slower. "So, all the hassle, all the pain, was because of one man's mistakes."

"Exactly. And I'm sorry, but your curiosity, vengeance, whatever, seems to have put you in the same position as Troy."

"And Fortner?" she pressed, trying to extend his conversation. Surely Saint had figured out something had delayed her.

"Fortner is being given another chance." Medium guy murmured, his eyes turning flat and dull. "One more. That's all I give."

"And my chance?" She ventured, hoping against hope that she'd leave the house alive.

"Sorry," he smiled and stood, then nodded at the man at the door. "I'll be waiting in the car."

Door guy nodded and watched as Medium walked out of the room, heading toward the back door. Celie heard the door close with a click and turned to stare at Door guy. He took a step closer and she closed her eyes and saw Saint's face, smiling and tender.

15

S aint looked out of the kitchen window, toward the side of the house. Nothing. He glanced at his watch. It had been over ten minutes since Celie left; where was she? He pulled his phone out and called North. "You see anything going on around the house or the one on the right?"

"No, why?"

"Celie went over to get her dad's dog a few minutes ago. She should be back by now."

"Which house is it?"

"The white one with blue shutters. Next door." Saint's gut roiled, his teeth clenched and his shoulder ached. Where the hell was she?

"I'll check it out." North clicked off.

Saint strode through the living room where Maggie and Anthony were both napping and went into the bedroom. "I'm going over to Maggie's house. Watch Anthony and Maggie."

He didn't give Bud any time to respond but turned and

left through the back door, texting North and South as he went.

Once outside the house, he hunkered down and tried to make himself as small as possible. Old habits borne in the desert and sands took over and he hustled to the low fence and knelt, his eyes on the house across the wooden slats.

It was quiet, with no movement in the yard. He opened the gate, wincing inwardly at the slight creak of the metal and crept through the space, leaving the gate open behind him. He'd just made it to the corner of the house when he saw the tall man, dressed in dark pants and shirt, edge around the opposite corner, a pistol at the ready. Saint lifted his gun then lowered it at the signal the other man gave. Two enemy combatants in the house. Saint nodded and signaled. Where? The other guy, North, he figured, pointed toward the other end of the house.

Saint took out his phone and showed it to North who nodded. Saint texted him, "South?"

"Front," North replied then, again with a signal, indicated he was going inside. Saint shook his head and pointed to the door and signaled stay. After a pause, North nodded. Saint texted him again to let South know to stay in front, in case. Again, North nodded.

As he approached the back door, Saint saw it open. He flattened himself on the ground as the storm door opened and a man dressed in jeans and a polo shirt came out. Saint cursed his position as he eyed the man, his back turned slightly away from him, walk down the single step and onto the concrete slab. Saint raised his pistol to fire only to see North tackle the man and take him down in near silence. As he delivered a blow to the man's head with his pistol butt, he nodded to the open doorway. "Go," he hissed.

Saint stepped into the kitchen, silent and sure. He heard

nothing over the sound of his breathing and eased the door shut with a click. With an urgency he didn't bother questioning, he ran with as much stealth as he could into the living room.

Celie knelt on the floor, her eyes closed and her hand on a dog lying at her side. A man on the other side of the room took a step toward her, leveling his pistol at her. Saint didn't think. He raised his gun and shot.

The guy went down, his leg giving out under him. Saint ran and kicked at his hand and the pistol flew from it, landing under a chair. Saint pointed his gun at the man's face, "If you fucking move, I'll kill you."

Eyes full of realization met his and the man leaned his head back and let out a breath, his hands resting on the floor.

Behind him, Saint heard a choked sob and Celie spoke, her voice hoarse. "There was another man—"

"We got him. He's outside. Call the police, baby."

She stood up beside him and, with a shaking hand, pulled her phone from her jeans and dialed 911. A few minutes later, she called her father's house.

"Who you talking to?"

"Maggie will know who to call about Sarge." She said faintly and then knelt again to caress the dog's side. "He's still breathing, believe it or not."

The siren, first faint and uneven, became louder and finally stopped outside the house. Saint remained where he was until a uniformed officer entered, his gun at the ready. "There's a man with pull ties around his wrists and ankles out back. You responsible for that?"

Saint lowered his gun and held his arms out at his sides as the officer took in the scene. "This man had a gun on her," Saint pointed to Celie who nodded. The officer glanced around the room, possibly for the gun before looking back at Saint. "I shot him in the leg to disarm him. The gun went under the couch or chair, I think."

Still holding his gun in their general direction, the cop bent and peered under the sofa then the chair. Straightening, he clicked his radio and asked for backup.

SAINT AND CELIE sat at Maggie's kitchen table and told, then retold their story. The detective cast a suspicious glance at both of them at first but when DEA agent Simpson entered the room, his face gleaming with satisfaction, the local police began to believe the pair. Hours later, their statements recorded and their presence no longer required, Saint and Celie walked hand in hand to her father's house where she spent half an hour arguing with her father that he did not, in fact, have to go to the vet hospital tonight. Sarge was being taken care of and Maggie, who'd jumped in and accompanied the dog, carried by Bud, to the hospital, would be happy to fill him in if he'd take the time to call her.

Anthony, alternately anxious and pissed that he'd missed the whole show, finally gave up and limped into his bedroom and slammed the door. Saint dropped onto the couch and eyed Celie, who stood before him, her jeans and hands stained with Sarge's blood. "You want to shower first?" He said and she nodded with a sigh.

"Except our clothes are still in the car."

"I'll go get them," he grinned and stood then wrapped her in his arms. "You were awesome, you know."

She snorted. "I was terrified and didn't do a damned thing to save myself."

He tightened his hold and she leaned her head against

his chest, wrapping her arms around his waist. "You kept yourself alive, baby. And that's what matters."

She lifted her head for a kiss, which lasted forever and only a second, then pulled away from him. "I want to wash this night off of me."

He nodded and went for the clothes. As he pulled the things from the car, his phone trilled and with a look, he answered. "Hey Hank. Thanks for the backup. They came in handy."

"So I heard. And Agent Simpson is about as happy as a man could be. You and Celie brought one of the head guys out of the dark. I think you may get a Christmas card from him."

Saint chuckled. "It turned out way better than I'd planned."

"You both were damned lucky." Hank hesitated then continued. "You think you and Celie might be up for a trip to Montana?"

Saint closed the hatch and leaned against the car. "For?"

"Your work on this case, while not strictly bodyguard, was pretty impressive. I was thinking you might want to make the practice permanent. And Celie, too, if she's interested."

Saint shouldered Celie's backpack and picked up his satchel with his left artificial hand and started toward the house. "Tell you what. We'll talk it over and I'll let you know what we decide. And Hank?"

"Yeah?"

"You gonna tell me who hired us to find and look after Celie?"

Hank hesitated for a minute then answered. "Simpson."

"Simpson?" Saint frowned, "How'd he figure in?"

"He'd become aware of her looking into things. He

figured if DEA or any other federal agency became involved, no one in the drug organization would come after Celie. By hiring us, he figured he'd protect her and maybe get some headway in the case."

He'd have to have a little talk with Agent Simpson, Saint thought. "You think we're out of the woods with the organization?"

"At least for now. With his arrest of Mitchell, that's the guy who was hogtied, Simpson will have an opportunity to get some good information. But, either way, you and Celie might stand to have some backup close at hand."

Saint stood at the back door, sounds of Celie talking to her father drifting into the evening. He'd talk to her. Both about the jobs and about their future together. "If we do decide to come to Montana, we'll be taking the long way. Celie kinda likes touring motels in small towns." He grinned, opened the door and headed into the house to find Celie.

The End

ABOUT THE AUTHOR

Kate McKeever was born and raised in Southern Appalachia and spent her formative years roaming the woods and reading, often at the same time. After over twenty years in occupational therapy, she is now happily retired and busy with her animals, her writing and her constant renovations to her old house.

OTHER BROTHERHOOD PROTECTORS
BOOKS BY KATE MCKEEVER

Saving Sidewinder

Sinner's Redemption

www.ingramcontent.com/pod-product-compliance
Lightning Source LLC
Chambersburg PA
CBHW071627140626
46555CB00021B/891